D0249670

GETTING LOST

GETTING LOST
ANNIE ERNAUX

Translated by Alison L. Strayer

Seven Stories Press
New York • Oakland

Seven Stories Press
140 Watts Street
New York, NY 10013
www.sevenstories.com

Library of Congress Cataloging-in-Publication Data

Names: Ernaux, Annie, 1940- author. | Strayer, Alison L., translator.
Title: Getting lost / Annie Ernaux ; translated by Alison L. Strayer.
Other titles: Se Perdre. English
Description: New York : Seven Stories Press, [2022] | "Originally published in French as Se Perdre (Paris: Gallimard, 2001)."
Identifiers: LCCN 2022013182 | ISBN 9781644212196 (trade paperback) | ISBN 9781644212202 (ebook)
Subjects: LCSH: Ernaux, Annie, 1940---Diaries. | Ernaux, Annie, 1940---Relations with men. | Middle-aged women--France--Diaries. | Man-woman relationships--France.
Classification: LCC PQ2665.R67 S413 2022 | DDC 843/.914--dc23/eng/20220708
LC record available at https://lccn.loc.gov/2022013182

College professors and high school and middle school teachers may order free examination copies of Seven Stories Press titles. Visit https://www.sevenstories.com/pg/resources-academics or email academics@sevenstories.com.

Printed in the United States of America

9 8 7 6 5 4 3 2 1

Voglio vivere una favola
(I want to live a fable)

Anonymous inscription on the steps of
the Basilica of Santa Croce, Florence

On Nov. 16, 1989, I phoned the Soviet embassy in Paris and asked to speak to Mr. S. The switchboard operator did not reply. After a long silence, a woman's voice said: "You know, Mr. S returned to Moscow yesterday." I immediately hung up. I felt as if I'd heard this sentence before, over the phone. The words were not the same but they had the same meaning, the same weight of horror, and were just as impossible to believe. Later, I remembered the announcement of my mother's death, three and a half years earlier, how the nurse at the hospital had said: "Your mother passed away this morning after breakfast."

The Berlin Wall had fallen several days before. The Soviet regimes established in Europe were toppling one after the other. The man who had just returned to Moscow was a faithful servant of the USSR, a Russian diplomat posted in Paris.

I had met him the previous year on a writers' junket to Moscow, Tbilisi, and Leningrad, a voyage he had been assigned to accompany. We had spent the last night together, in Leningrad. After returning to France, we continued to see each other. The ritual was invariable. He would ring to ask if he could come around to see me in the afternoon or evening, or, more rarely, a day or two later. He would arrive and stay just a few hours, which we spent making love. Then he left, and I would live in wait for his next call.

He was thirty-five. His wife worked as his secretary at the embassy. His trajectory, which I pieced together over the course of our meetings, was typical of a young apparatchik: membership in the Komsomol and then in the CPSU (Communist Party of the Soviet Union), time spent in Cuba. He spoke French quickly, with a strong accent. Though outwardly a partisan of Gorbachev and perestroika, when he'd had a drink, he mourned the time of Brezhnev and made no secret of his veneration of Stalin.

I never knew anything about his activities, which, officially, were related to culture. Today, I am amazed that I did not ask more questions. Nor will I ever know what I meant to him. His desire for me was the only thing I was sure of. He was, in every sense of the word, the shadow lover.

During this period, I wrote nothing but the articles which I was asked to do for magazines. The only place where I truly wrote was in the journal I had kept, on and off, since adolescence. It was a way of enduring the wait until we saw each other again, of heightening the pleasure by recording the words and acts of passion. Most of all, it was a way to save life, save from nothingness the thing that most resembles it.

After he left France, I started to write a book about this passion which had swept through me and continued to live inside me. I worked on the book sporadically, finished it in 1991, and published it in 1992 as *Simple Passion*.

In the spring of 1999, I traveled to Russia again. I had not been back since my trip in 1988. I did not see S, but this made no difference to me. In Leningrad, which had become Saint Petersburg again, I could not recall the name of the hotel where I had spent the night with him. During the visit, the only trace that remained of this passion was my knowledge of a few words of Russian. Exhaustingly, and in spite of myself, I continually tried to decipher the Cyrillic script on signs and billboards. It surprised me that I knew those words, that alphabet. The man for whom I had learned them had ceased to exist in me, and I no longer cared whether he was alive or dead.

In January or February 2000, I started to reread my journals from the year of my passionate affair with S. It had been five years since I had opened them. (For reasons that need not be specified here, they had been stored in a place that made them unavailable to me.) I perceived there was a "truth" in those pages that differed from the one to be found in *Simple Passion*—something raw and dark, without salvation, a kind of *oblation*. I thought that this, too, should be brought to light.

I neither altered nor removed any part of the original text while typing it into the computer. For me, words set down on paper to capture the thoughts and sensations of a given moment are as irreversible as time—are time itself. I simply used initials when expressing a judgment that I felt could harm the person to whom they referred, and also to designate the object of my passion, S. Not that I believe that in doing so, I could protect his identity—a vain illusion, if there ever was one—but because the de-realizing effect of the initial seemed consistent with what this man was to me: the embodiment of the absolute, of something which instills a *nameless terror*.

The outside world is almost totally absent from these pages. To this day, I continue to feel it was more important to record daily thoughts and actions, the things which constitute the novel of life that a love affair is (details from the socks he did not remove while making love to his desire to die at the wheel of his car), rather than the current events of the period, which can always be checked in archives.

I am conscious that I am publishing this journal because of an inner imperative, without concern for how S might feel. He could rightly judge it an abuse of literary power, or even a betrayal. I could understand if he defends himself with laughter or disdain: "I only saw her to get my rocks off." But I would rather that he accept (even if he doesn't understand) that for months, without knowing it, he embodied the principle, wondrous and terrifying, of desire, of death and writing.

Autumn 2000

1988

September
Tuesday 27

S . . . the beauty of it all: the very same desires, the same actions as at other times in the past, in '58 and '63, and with P. The same drowsiness, even torpor. Three scenes stand out. That evening (Sunday) in his room, as we sat close to each other, touching, saying nothing, willing and eager for what would follow, which still depended on me. His hand passed close to my legs, stretched out in front of me, and brushed them each time he put his cigarette ash in the container on the floor. In front of everyone. We talked as if nothing were going on. Then the others leave (Marie R, Irène, RVP) but F hangs back, waiting to leave with me. I know that if I leave S's room now, I won't have the strength to return. Then everything's a blur. F is outside the room, or almost, the door is open, and it seems to me that S and I throw ourselves at each other. Then the door is closed (by whom?) and we are just inside, in the entry hall. My back, pressed against the wall, switches the light off and on. I have to move aside. I drop my raincoat, handbag, suit jacket. S turns off the light. The night begins, which I experience with absolute intensity (along with the desire never to see him again, as with other men in the past).

The second moment, Monday afternoon. When I've finished packing my case, he knocks at the door to my room. We caress each other in the doorway. He wants me so much that I kneel down and lingeringly make him come with my mouth. He is silent, then only murmurs my name like a litany, with his Russian accent. My back pressed against the wall—darkness (he doesn't want the lights on)—communion.

The third moment is on the sleeper train for Moscow. We kiss at the back of the carriage, my head next to a fire extinguisher (which I only identify later). All this happened in Leningrad.

I feel no sense of caution or restraint, nor do I have any doubts, finally. Something has come full circle. I commit the same errors as in the past but they are no longer errors. There is only beauty, passion, desire.

Since my flight home yesterday, I have tried to reconstruct events, but they tend to elude me, as if something had happened outside my consciousness. All I am sure of is that on Saturday, in Zagorsk, as we visit the Treasures in the monastery, slippers on our feet, he takes me by the waist for a few seconds, and I know right away that I will agree to sleep with him. But what was the state of my desire later? There was a meal with Chetverikov, the director of the VAAP [All-Union Agency on Copyrights], and S is seated at a distance. We leave for Leningrad by sleeper train. I desire him then, but we can't do anything, and I don't worry about it: I don't care at this point whether it happens or not. Sunday, we visit Leningrad, Dostoevsky's house in the morning. I think I've been wrong about his attraction to me and think of it no more (am I sure about that?). Meal at the Hotel Europe: I'm seated next to him, but that has happened many times since the beginning of the trip. (One day, in Georgia, when he was seated next to me, I spontaneously wiped my wet hands on his jeans.) On the visit to the Hermitage, we're not together much. Crossing a bridge over the Neva on the way back, we're together, leaning on the parapet with our elbows. Dinner at the Hotel Karelia: I am seated apart from him. RVP eggs him on to get Marie to dance. It's a slow number. Yet I know he has the same desire as me. (I have just forgotten an episode: the ballet, before dinner. Sitting beside him, I can think of nothing but my desire for him, especially during the second part of the performance: *The Three Musketeers*, Broadway-style. I've still got the music in my head. I tell myself that if I can remember the name of Louis-Ferdinand Céline's companion, a dancer, we'll sleep together. I remember, it's Lucette Almanzor.) In his room, where he's invited us to come drink vodka, he visibly arranges things so as to be sitting next to me. Great difficulty in ousting F, who fancies me and wants to be near me too. And then I know, I feel it, I am sure. It's the perfect sequence of moments: our connection, the strength of a desire that has had little need for words, the great beauty of it. The few seconds' separation which ignites the fusion by the door. We clutch each other, kissing as if to die from it. He tears my mouth, my tongue from me, crushes me against him.

Seven years after my first trip to the USSR, I have a revelation about my relation to men (that is, my relations with one particular man, with him, not another, as with Claude G and then Philippe in the past). The immense fatigue. S is thirty-six (he looks thirty), is slim, and tall (next to him, in heels, I am petite), with green eyes and light brown hair. The last time I thought of P was in bed, after making love—faint sorrow. Now all I think about is seeing S again, and living this passion to the limit. And like Philippe in '63, S will return to Paris on September 30.

Thursday 29

Sometimes I can picture his face, but only fleetingly. There, now, I've lost it again. I know his eyes, the shape of his lips, his teeth, but they do not form a whole. Only his body is identifiable—his hands, not yet. I am consumed with desire, to the point of tears. I want perfection in love, as I believe I attained a kind of perfection in writing with *A Woman's Story.* That can only happen through giving, while throwing all caution to the wind. I'm already well on my way.

Friday 30

He hasn't called yet. I don't know what time his plane gets in. He is part of that lineage of tall, blond, and slightly shy men who marked the course of my youth and whom I always sent packing in the end. But now I know that only they can put up with me and make me happy. How to explain the strange, silent accord of that Sunday in Leningrad, if it's all meant to end? Deep down, I don't believe it's possible for us *not* to see each other. The question is when.

October
Saturday 1

It was a quarter to one. His flight was three hours late. Painful happiness. It really makes no difference if he calls or not, the excruciating tension is the same. I've known this since the age of sixteen (with G de V, Claude G, Philippe—the three main ones—and then with P). Is this the beginning of a "beautiful love story"? I am afraid to die on the road between Lille and Paris tonight, afraid of anything that could keep me from seeing him again.

Sunday 2

Fatigue, torpor. Slept four hours after my return from Lille. Made love for two hours in David's studio (David and Éric are my two sons). Bruises, pleasure, and the constant awareness of making the most of these moments, before the departure, before desire wanes. Before the terrible threat of "I'm too old." But at thirty-five, I could have been jealous of a beautiful woman of fifty.

Parc de Sceaux, the ponds and canal, cold damp weather, the smell of earth. In '71, when I was here to pass the *agrégation,** I never would have guessed that I'd return to this park with a Soviet diplomat. (As it is, I've already pictured myself going back in a few years to retrace the steps of today's walk, as I did a month ago in Venice, in memory of '63.)

He likes fancy cars, luxury, social connections, and isn't much of an intellectual. This too is a step back in time, to the hateful image of my husband, but even that now appears to me in a pleasant light, because it corresponds to a part of my past. I'm not even afraid in the car with him.

How do I go about this so that my attachment doesn't show too quickly and so that the difficulty of keeping me becomes apparent to him, at least once in a while?

Monday 3

Last night, he called. I was sleeping. He wanted to come around. Not possible. (Éric here.) Restless night, what to do

---

* The highest teaching diploma in France.

with this desire? The same goes for today, when again I won't see him. I weep from desire, this all-consuming hunger for him. He represents the most "parvenu" part of myself, the most adolescent too. He's not very intellectual, loves fancy cars, music while he drives. He likes to "make a splash." He's that "man of my youth," blond and unrefined (his hands, his square fingernails), who fills me with pleasure (and whom I no longer wish to reproach for his lack of intellectualism). Nonetheless, I really need to catch up on my sleep now. I'm at the point of total exhaustion, unable to do anything. Love and mourning are one and the same for me, in body and in mind.

Song by Edith Piaf: *Mon Dieu, laissez le-moi, encore un peu, un jour, deux jours, un mois, le temps de s'adorer et de souffrir . . .** The longer I live, the more I abandon myself to love. The illness and death of my mother revealed the strength of my need for the other. When I say, "I love you" to S, I am amused to hear him reply, "Thank you!" which is not so very far from "Thank you, think nothing of it!" And he says to me with happiness and pride, "You'll see my wife!" As for me, I'm the writer, the foreigner, the whore—the free woman too. I'm not the "good woman," whom one possesses and displays, the one who gives consolation. I can't console anyone.

Tuesday 4

I don't know if he wants us to continue. "Diplomatic" illness, he says (laughs!). I'm on the verge of tears, for the party

---

* "Oh God, leave him with me, just a little longer, one day, two days, a month . . . give us the time to worship each other and to suffer . . ."

is not happening. How often have I waited, got ready, made myself "beautiful" and welcoming, and then—nothing. It did not happen. And for me he's so impenetrable, mysterious by necessity, and probably full of deceit by nature. He's been with the Party since '79. Proud, as if it were a step up in life, an exam he passed: he is among the finest servants of the Soviet Union.

My only scrap of happiness all day: being hit on in the RER by a young lout, and producing the right lingo, which came to my lips spontaneously: "Keep that up and I'll knock your lights out!" etc. Oh, to be the heroine of a squalid little pickup attempt in a deserted RER, with two stooges looking on.

Is the happiness with S already over?

Wednesday 5

Nine o'clock, last night, a call . . . "I'm here, close by, in Cergy . . ." He came around and we spent two hours shut into my study, as David is here. This time, there is no restraint on his part. Later, I could not sleep, could not detach myself from his body, which remained inside me. That's my whole drama, I'm unable to forget the other, to be autonomous. I soak up other people's words and actions, my body absorbs the other body. It's so difficult to work after a night like this.

Thursday 6

Last night, he collected me in Cergy and we went to David's studio on rue Lebrun. Semi-darkness, his body both visible and veiled. The usual madness for nearly three hours. On our return he drove quickly, with the radio playing ("En rouge et noir," a hit from last year), flashing the headlights off and on. He shows me the powerful car he wants to buy. He's the perfect parvenu, a little boorish ("The holidays aren't over yet, we can still hook up," he says . . .). Misogynistic, too: women in politics are hilarious, women are terrible drivers, etc. And it's me who revels in it . . . my strange pleasure in it all. More and more I see in him "the man of my youth," the ideal I described in *Cleaned Out*. After we've arrived at the gate in front of the house, there is one final scene, a superb enactment (it feels to me) of that thing called love, for want of another word: he leaves the radio on (Yves Duteil, "Le petit pont de bois") and I stroke him with my mouth until he comes, there, in the car, in the allée des Lozères. Afterwards, we lose ourselves in each other's eyes. This morning when I wake up, I go over the scene interminably. He's been back in France for less than a week, and already we're so attached, so free with each other's bodies (we have done almost everything that can be done), compared to how we were in Leningrad. I've always made love and always written as if I were going to die afterwards (moreover, I longed for an accident, for death, as we were driving back to my place on the motorway last night).

Friday 7

Desire not exhausted but continually renewed, with greater pain and power. I can no longer picture his face when he's not here. Even when I'm with him, I see him differently from before. He has another face, so close, so irrefutable, like a double. I almost always take the lead, but in accordance with his desires.

Last night, I was sleeping when he phoned, which often happens. Tension, happiness, desire. My name murmured with that guttural accent which palatalizes and emphasizes the first syllable, making the second one very short (*aân'i*). No one will ever say my name that way again.

I remember my arrival in Moscow, in 1981 (around October 9), the Russian soldier, so tall, so young, I burst into tears, overwhelmed to be there, in that near-imaginary country. Now it is a little as if I were making love with that Russian soldier and all the emotion of seven years ago had led to S. One week ago, I did not foresee this conflagration. André Breton wrote, "We made love as the sun beats, as coffins close"—that pretty much describes us.

Saturday 8

The studio on rue Lebrun. Slight weariness at first, then sweetness and exhaustion. At one point, he said, "I'll call you next week"—in other words, "I don't want to see you over the weekend." I smile—in other words, I accept. There is suffering and jealousy on my part, though I know very well it's best to plan slightly longer intervals between meetings. I am back in the "day-after" state of disarray. I'm afraid of seeming clingy and old (clingy because old), and wonder if I shouldn't play the separation card, double or nothing!

Tuesday 11

He left at 11:00 p.m. It's the first time I've made love for so many hours in a row, without a lull. At ten thirty he gets up. Me: Would you like anything? Him: Yes, you. Back to the bedroom. How difficult things will be at the end of October, which marks the end of our meetings, with the arrival of his wife. But will he be able to give them up as easily as that? He seems to me quite attached to the pleasure we have together. To hear him excoriate sexual freedom and pornography, and the philandering habits of the Georgians! Now he dares to ask me, "Did you come?" He didn't in the beginning. Tonight, anal sex for the first time. Good that the first time was with him. It's true that a young man in one's bed takes the mind off time and age. This need for a man is so terrible, so close to a desire for death, an annihilation of self, how long can it go on . . .

Wednesday 12

My mouth, face, and sex are ravaged. I don't make love like a writer, that is, in a removed way, or while thinking, "I can use this in a book." I always make love as if it were the last time (and who's to say it isn't?), simply as a living being.

Think: in Leningrad, he was so awkward (due to shyness? or relative inexperience?). He's becoming less and less so. Am I then, in some sense, an initiatrix? The role enchants me, but it is fragile and ambiguous. It holds no promise of longevity (he could push me away like a whore). His blitheness and contradictions amuse me: he talks about his wife, how they met, and the necessary restrictions on morality in the USSR, and minutes later, begs to go upstairs so we can make love. What happiness this is. And naturally his joy was palpable when I said, "You're such a good lover!" But I liked it too, in Leningrad, when he said something similar to me.

Thursday 13

Here, mention should be made of the constant interplay between love and the desire for clothes, insatiable, though I suspect futile with regard to desire in general. It was the same in '84, when I continually bought skirts, pullovers, dresses, etc. never looking at the price—spending as if there were no tomorrow.

This waiting for the phone to ring, in addition to his total inscrutability—what do I mean to him?

And I'm starting to learn Russian!

Saturday 15

At the foot of the stairs, rue Lebrun: he doesn't knock and tries to enter. I turn the key. A soft, smooth body, not very manly, except for . . . And he's tall, much taller than me. That gesture he has of turning out the light before we make love, interminably. Taking me home, he drives very quickly, my hand on his thigh—the stereotype. Love/death, but oh so intense.

Last Tuesday, when I was near La Défense, I thought about how much I love the world of the city, this landscape of tower blocks, of lights and even cars—faceless, crowded places, the site of meetings and passions, past and present (Le Mail in Yvetot, empty Sundays, quiet as the grave, "will I ever get out of this place?" . . .).

In any case, S is already a beautiful love story (and it's only been three weeks).

Monday 17

Always presume indifference. Today, I'm certain that nothing more will come of this after the end of October, and it may even end before. It occurred to me that I hadn't asked his wife's name (a subtle form of jealousy, or the desire to annihilate the other woman).

Tuesday 18/Wednesday 19

1:30 a.m. He left at a quarter to one, having come back with me from Paris at eight thirty. He makes love (or rather, we do) with desire that is more and more acute and profound. He talks, drinks vodka, and we make love again, etc. . . . three times in four hours. My Tuesdays rival those of rue de Rome (I'm talking about Mallarmé—and myself, with P). Naturally, there's very little thinking, or more precisely, thought goes no further than the present: flesh and the Other. At every instant, I *am* this elusive present—in the car, in bed, in the living room when we talk. Uncertainty gives these meetings an unbridled, violent intensity.

Over the day that follows, I remain entangled with this presence. In lightning images, I see us making love the night before (he tells me to turn around, he's on his back and moans as I caress him with my mouth, he says "You make incredible love" and gently guides me to his lower belly, taking the initiative at last). Then memory and numbness evaporate, and I need him again, but I'm alone. The waiting resumes. I don't see when I'm going to work (on my courses or a book), unless it ends.

Friday 21

No word since Tuesday evening. Never knowing why. Waiting.

Feverishly working in the garden. A few hours more and it will be too late for us to meet in Paris tonight. I haven't wept, not even once, since the affair began. Maybe I will tonight, if we don't see each other.

Saturday 22

I'm leaving for Marseille with still no word from him. Tears last night, of course. I wake up at 2:00 a.m. in pain and not caring if I die, even wishing for death. Then my thoughts of death are replaced by thoughts of writing, the idea that I could write about "this person" and our meetings. And I understand that desire, writing and death have always been interchangeable for me. And so yesterday a phrase from my book about my mother came back to me: "The worst moments were when I left home . . ." I could have said the same of that day when all love seemed lost. I know that *Cleaned Out* was written on a backdrop of pain and ruined union. I know that between Philippe and me, there was death: the abortion. I write in lieu of love, to fill that empty space above death. I make love with the same desire for perfection that I feel in relation to writing.

Dreamed that I stole (in order to drive) the Renault Alpine that we had nine years ago. Such a clear symbol, that car: an object of seduction for S, who is wild about fast and "classy" rides. What misunderstanding. All that attracts him is my status as a writer, my "glory," and all those things that are built on my suffering, my failure at living, the very forces at play in our relationship.

Sunday 23

This morning, I'm almost alone at the Deux Garçons café in Aix-en-Provence. A memory of Bordeaux in 1963. My love of cafés, anonymity, chance encounters. The pain and unease are the same as in '63. No word from him since Tuesday night. No idea what's going on. Such indifference from him, obviously, makes me fear the worst. He called me at night. Two weeks, and already so remote. In the TGV,* desire for him so strong I could have screamed. Tirelessly, I go over our last time together, every action, every word (the words so rare). At eighteen I was mad and wanted to die. I no longer feel the same despair.

Monday 24

11:10 p.m., phone call for a Wednesday meeting (maybe). Obviously, these nocturnal things are less momentous for him than for me. I have too much time to think of passion, that is my misfortune. No absolutely mandatory tasks are imposed on me from outside. Freedom makes me prone to passion, so very occupying.

Wednesday, lunch with the Soviet ambassador, Riabov, and the president of the VAAP. S is bound to be present, a situa-

---

* *Train à Grande Vitesse*, the high-speed train.

tion both awkward and exciting. For him to come to me that evening, after a public ceremony where we've appeared utterly indifferent to each other, would be perfection. There is an inexhaustible charm to secrecy.

Tuesday 25

In the morning, I daydream on and on, imagining things which in two days will be behind me. Then I have trouble focusing on what I'm doing in the present. Insofar as my daydreams are not gratuitous and are destined to come true, they're already part of reality. Though come to think of it, and this surprises me, the reality of the past may be more wonderful (such as Leningrad). I want tomorrow to attain a kind of perfection, but it may be a catastrophe—a boring meal, the impossibility of our seeing each other in the evening. In any case, I'm going to wear a black suit, a green blouse and a string of pearls, the one I left on while making love (if he recognizes them when we're at the table). I know I've never been as beautiful as now, more than at twenty or thirty—everyone tells me so, and men constantly hit on me, it happened again yesterday at Auchan. The swan song (and the ballet we saw in Leningrad was *Swan Lake*). Now I remember what happened in the room in Leningrad. I went to leave, was just about to close the door behind me, and then I stepped back in. He must have been right there, because we immediately flung ourselves at each other.

Wednesday 26

How to describe the joy of that lunch? Of his being there across from me. Of knowing I'd see him in the evening, knowing we are lovers but letting nothing show (in fact, maybe not showing enough for my taste). It's eight o'clock. He should be here in an hour or two. These hours of waiting are the end of the world—great happiness not yet brought to completion. Pre-happiness. That is, I know that anything can happen, that he may not come, there could be an accident. Piaf's song: *Mon Dieu! Mon Dieu! Mon Dieu! Laissez-le-moi encore un peu . . . Même si j'ai tort, laissez-le-moi encore.** So much beauty and desire. Erase October '63, clumsy, appallingly clumsy youth.

Thursday 27

It's about twenty to ten. He left at a quarter to three in the morning. "I drove like a madman." I can no longer isolate any detail of this part of a night spent together. Making love indefatigably, bodies (but is it the body? what is that thing whose hunger outruns desire?) never separated, or so little. And it felt like a last time, although he wants to see me again, in spite of his wife.

In one month, we've gone from inept sex to a kind of perfection—well, almost. He resists sentiment, and it has to be that way (what would I do with a man who wanted to change my life?), but not sensual attachment. He's more willing to "give"

---

* "My God, leave him with me just a little longer . . . Even if it's wrong of me, leave him with me just a little longer."

now, as I yearn to give, though he retains a certain brutality, signifying lack of experience. I sense he is really discovering what sex can be and wants to do *everything* (hence his request to make love between the breasts, my breasts). He left and I slept with a sensation of being inside his body.

Wednesday, October 26, was a perfect day.

He listed: his Saint Laurent shirt, his Saint Laurent sports jacket, his Cerruti tie, Ted Lapidus trousers. A craving for luxury, for things they lack in the USSR. As a former ill-clad adolescent, consumed with longing for the rich girls' dresses, how can I blame him? And it seemed to me that all those clothes of his were new, and that he wants to dress even more smartly. The courtship display. All this, too, is beautiful.

My name in the night, a lament of pleasure. My adoration of his sex. I think of a painting, the naked Christ lifted down from the cross, when S half-raises himself to watch me caress him with my mouth (he didn't do this at the beginning), and revels in the image of my adoration. The curve of his chest, of his loins, the whiteness of his skin in the semi-darkness. I'm so tired . . . unable to do anything but write about him, about "that thing," so mysterious and so terrible.

Now, I no longer seek truth in love, but the perfection of a relationship, beauty and pleasure. Avoid saying things that wound, in other words, only say things he will like. Also avoid anything which, though true, would present an unflattering image of me. Truth can only rule in writing, not in life.

I went to La Rochelle. Clear skies on Sunday, the opening of the port. On the train, I tried to read, obsessed with the fact that his wife is about to arrive. Last night, he called at around half past midnight, wanting to see me this week, Monday or Tuesday. And then, after his call, I said aloud, several times, "What joy!" What joy to have heard his voice and know that things aren't over. This afternoon, I thought about the day in December, at age sixteen, when, in order to meet G de V, I managed to soldier on in class for a whole day with a fever of 39 degrees, and was prepared to go to the cinema the following day with a fever of 40 degrees. Then he couldn't go. I went home, got into bed, and fought pneumonia for two weeks. I haven't changed. I just can't do it for quite so long, perhaps (I mean, I can't persist for quite so long in that kind of folly). What I wrote to S is true: "It's as if there had never been anyone before you."

November
Tuesday 1st

Yesterday afternoon, we met at the studio on rue Lebrun, so things were less private (the neighbors' TV). He arrives, chilled to the bone by this first day of cold (0 degrees). He wears a very Soviet-looking singlet. I see his ragged fingernails (there's always that uncouth side, observed at the ambassador's residence, common to Soviets). And for me these traits are more endearing than anything I can think of. Afterwards, I go to Héloïsa and Carlos Freire's. José Artur is there (I didn't know he would be) and I arrive exhausted, emanating a powerful odor of male, my face bruised and blotched with kisses (it is a fact, it shows, I have red patches on my chin). All my pain lies in this: no sooner have I seen him, and recovered from our (almost nonstop) lovemaking, than I am anxious to see him again. But November cannot repeat our shimmering October, because his wife has arrived. Also because passion inexorably abates.

Something I recalled last night: for several months, in my room in Yvetot, I kept the blood-stained underpants from the night in September '58, in Sées. Basically, I am "redeeming" '58, the horror of those last three months of '58 on which my life is built, transposed (not very well) in *Ce qu'ils disent ou rien*.*

Friday, Friday . . . Meeting his wife a horrifying prospect. I have to be the most beautiful of all, the one who sparkles most, desperately.

Wednesday 2

I always dream of something more, and therefore of exclusive meetings in the Nièvre or elsewhere, etc., unable to be satisfied by the repetition of current relations. (No doubt that's why I wanted to marry Philippe, not suspecting that it would put an end to the dream.)

Evening. It's been a week. My feeling, then, that nothing will ever be so powerful again. I fear this more and more. He won't

---

* Annie Ernaux's first novel, yet to be translated into English (the title translates as *Whatever They Say Goes*).

be able to come to Cergy at night anymore. The studio repels me with its lighting and the racket from the neighbors.

The feeling that it will all slowly end. I don't speak his language. He never calls me except to make love (I was going to say "fuck," it's more to the point). But at the embassy on Friday, there'll at least be the satisfaction of secrecy, of what we know about each other, the other's body, breath, the buried animal, all that for me is the essential that others cannot guess at. The October Revolution! Were those tears on my arrival in Moscow in '81 prophetic?

Friday 4

The anniversary of the October Revolution . . . A sad little crowd from the Soviet embassy, the "bunker." S asks, "Can I come around this afternoon?" I hadn't expected this, hence the lack of waiting and dreaming. Does he feel as much desire as me? I don't know, I think so. Beautiful weather, I close the shutters and his body is returned to me, desire refined, perfected before love.

Anxiety about the dinner at the Élysée on Monday with Charles and Diana. So it will never end, there'll always be something even more daunting than the latest society event? The ordeal of the most recent Gallimard lunch, with F. Mitterrand, will be outdone?

A new notebook. Wishes: to have a stronger and stronger relationship with S; to write (as I yearn to do) a bigger, more sweeping book, starting at the beginning of '89; to not have money problems.

Monday 7

Obviously it was for S that I agreed to go to dinner at the Élysée tonight, to increase my worth in terms of the thing he most venerates: visible glory.

I consider this "must" event a test, a necessary challenge. It means going to the height of social distinction, of something that was not a dream but a reality from which I knew myself to be excluded, at age sixteen (in '56, by some strange coincidence, while ill, in bed, I read *Le Figaro* and suffered from the knowledge that G de V moved in those kinds of circles, of which I was utterly "unworthy").

Tuesday 8

This time, for once, I truly yearned to experience pomp, the highest honors. My raging anxiety at being late, the fear of not getting there on time to be "in the mix," weaving in and out of traffic in the Renault 5 down the Champs-Élysées and avenue de Marigny. Was Prince Charles *real* to me? The royal dinner, music . . . It crossed my mind that this old-world "entente cordiale" may one day be swept away by other powers—I was thinking of the USSR and China. Perhaps last night we resembled the people of 1913 or 1938, gathered in these same gilded halls—or, fleetingly, those at Madame Bovary's dinner in Vaubyessard. For me, none of it holds a candle to the desire for a man, or the night in Leningrad. And if I dream of a return to Moscow (which is probably madness) at the end of November, at the same time as Mitterrand (who remembered very well that we'd talked about Venice at the Gallimard lunch: "Last summer,

I went to Venice and thought of you," he said), it would only be to "present" this honor to S, to make him love me. Yet I know that often love has no use for all this (so the kind of honors which would so gratify S would only be a bore for me).

S was born on April 6, '53. My mother died on April 7. Éric was conceived on April 2.

Again I long to see him. And yet what it all comes down to is this: he fucks, he drinks vodka, he talks about Stalin.

I have a completely different relationship with time than in the old days, or when I was with P. Each time S and I meet, I know that something new and terribly intense has been added to our relationship that will necessarily drive us apart. The current lucidity, the absence of suffering (or rather, stifled suffering) puts me face to face with time, more squarely than before.

I picture him as a middle-aged man, with a bit of a paunch, gray at the temples. What will I have become in his memory?

Thursday 10

Yesterday, Yvetot. As soon as I get there, I cry. I wrote in *A Woman's Story*: "She spent all day selling milk and potatoes so that I could sit in a lecture hall and learn about Plato." And yesterday I thought: "They lived and died so that I could attend a reception at the Élysée . . ." A story is never finished. I learned yesterday from my aunts that my mother had met a "good" man in Annecy and thought about remarrying. Now I know why she went to see a psychic: there was a future still, at sixty-five, beyond that even. This both disturbs and pleases me. I am the daughter of a woman who was full of desire she dared not take to its limit.

But I do. I'm waiting for S now. Éric's presence is unbearable. He stays until the last minute, keeping me from dreaming and waiting. There's always the dread of seeing love fade.

Evening. No, it's still as strong as ever. I regret having shown him the beginning of this journal. Never say anything, never show too much love: Proust's law of desire. S knows it instinctively. But I saw that he returned the passion, with some help from the half bottle of vodka he drank. He will probably leave in a year. He says, "It will be hard." At the beginning, I don't quite understand but he adds: "I hope it will be hard for you too." And that's his way of saying he cares about me. We made love for hours. Again, something's different. He talks more, dares to say erotic words. All his gestures are love, like mine.

Friday 11

As on all the other nights when he has been here, I cannot sleep—I'm still inside his skin, his male gestures. Today, again, I'll be caught between fusion and the return to self. And there are always separate moments that emerge from the whole that is the evening. His words in the kitchen, "It will be hard," then his eyes as he sits in the armchair, before he leaves. The time before, in the bedroom, his gentleness, the erotic words he spoke with his Russian accent, his murmuring, "You are beautiful."

Write this: I realized that I'd lost a contact lens. I found it on his penis. (I thought of Zola, who lost his monocle between the breasts of women—and now I my contact lens on my lover's sex!)

I compare the way things are now with the night in Leningrad, how he's changed, how awkward he was then. I think the word for it now is passion.

Saturday 12

Four years ago, it was the Renaudot prize.* I prefer it to be now, to be in this perpetual state of waiting and desire. I had the urge to reconstruct the trip to the USSR, which I surely never would have done had the trip not ended with my meeting S.

Sunday, September 18, evening. The car whose windshield wipers didn't work, rock music playing full blast in the car that takes us from the airport to the Hotel Rossia. The night is freezing cold. I can see the Moskva from my window.

Monday 19, Narodna Cultura. Meeting at the Central House of Writers. Lunch. A walk around Red Square with RVP, Marie R, Alain N, coming back through the gardens. I can see us all in those deserted places. Departure for Tbilisi (S sits next to me on the plane, which disturbs me, for I'd like to sleep). Evening in Tbilisi: on the sixteenth floor, as a lampoon, we inaugurate Cohiba Cell 16!

Tuesday 20. Visit to Tbilisi, the suspended church
    Lunch at the hotel
    Museum
    Translation school
    Film *Don Quixote*, S next to me
Wednesday 21. Various meetings
    Monastery, ancient capital

---

* In November 1984, Annie Ernaux was presented with the Prix Renaudot for *La place* (*A Man's Story*).

Return to Moscow. Hotel of the CPSU central committee
Thursday 22. Kremlin tour
   Circus
   Dinner at the home of the correspondent for *L'Humanité*
Friday 23. TV in the morning
   Lunch at the French embassy
   Various meetings
   Arbat Street
Saturday 24. Zagorsk
   Lunch in the Museum
   Meal at VAAP headquarters
   Departure for Leningrad by train
Sunday 25. Dostoevsky's house
   Hotel lunch (S next to me)
   The Hermitage
   Ballet
   Dinner at the hotel, with orchestra.

Tuesday 15

The wait begins as soon as I wake up. There is never any
"after." Life stops from the moment he rings the doorbell
and enters. I'm tormented by the fear that he won't be able
to come. The beauty of this whole affair lies in its continual
uncertainty. But I don't know the nature of his attachment.
To say that it is "sensual" doesn't mean anything. Anyway,
that would be the most beautiful, truest, and clearest kind of
attachment.

4:00 p.m. I'll remember these magnificent sun-filled afternoons in November, waiting for S, for the sound of his car that

heralds our entry into that other time in which time disappears, replaced by desire.

Midnight. A crazy night. He had too much to drink. At half past ten, the car wouldn't start. Stupid, dangerous maneuvers. I beg him to wait until the engine is no longer flooded. He cannot stand, or not very well. He wants to make love in the hallway, then the kitchen. Upside-down, very interesting—the ludicrous acrobatics of man and woman, meant to signify love, to *enact it*, over and over again.

Even more desire. He said "my love" once but will not say "I love you," and that which remains unsaid does not exist. I'm afraid he won't get home safely, that he'll have an accident. Must prevent him from drinking so much the next time, if there is one—the traditional superstition. We are under the rule of passion.

Wednesday 16

Yesterday, as usual, a slight taste of the abject. The last time we went upstairs: the acrid smell of beer, him saying, "Help me" (to ejaculate). Then after the car trouble, once more, in the vestibule, half-dressed, against the radiator, and in the kitchen. He was visibly drunk, French words escaped him, and he'd almost ceased to speak, simply wanted me.

Earlier, he'd talked about his childhood, and about Siberia, where he worked on log drives. About the bears roaming free. He is somewhat, not to say very, anti-Semitic: "Isn't Mitterrand Jewish?" (!) It's as if I were unable to believe it, putting it down to sheer indoctrination, for which he cannot be held responsible.

I am afraid that he'll waken from the "hell of the senses" (hitherto unknown to him) we are plummeting into. After yesterday, there isn't much left of the Kama Sutra for us to do. He knows ahead of time what I've imagined us doing—it's quite astonishing. Surely he must do research? In books, or erotic films?

He adheres to the dogma of "nature," like the writers Rasputin and Astafiev: "Love, alcohol—only natural!"

Last night, his face was that of a suffering child, the face of boundless inextinguishable desire. At moments such as these, I know that I still have him.

I have just reread the proofs of *Ce qu'ils disent ou rien* for the pocket edition. I hadn't read the book in eleven years. I haven't changed, I'm still that girl who believes in happiness, who waits and suffers. This book, written in a very conversational style, is much more profound (with regard to words and the real) than the critics said.

Thursday 17

The cycle begins again: a doleful, lethargic day when I'm unable to do anything creative. Then the waiting returns, the desire, and the suffering, because in the type of relationship we have, I'm at the mercy of his phone calls. And I have to write about the Revolution. Horrible. And I still don't know how he got home on Tuesday evening, or if his wife noticed anything, or if he "talked"—the worst possibility of all. Right now my life has no other future than the next phone call in the night. His death would be an atrocity from which I'm not sure I could recover. Since yesterday (this morning, especially), I have been in a state of acute anxiety because of the way in which he left, during the night on Tuesday. He was really drunk. I have a mad longing to ring the embassy. Won't do it, obviously. I'm really in love.

Friday 18

Woke at half past four and thought, "He didn't call" (in the night, as he sometimes does). Time marches on—only two weeks since the reception at the embassy for the October Revolution! I was so anxious, then, about meeting his wife, who did not come in the end. The present is so powerful, so riveting, that the future and past seem light years away.

He "should" call tonight. He usually does three days after our last meeting. But in this situation, routine and regularity are not really the norm.

Saturday 19

I really ask myself, must I continue to live this way, between expectation and chagrin, apathy and desire? Complete similarity between my behavior at the time of my mother's death and now: I'm always doing something for him (as I did then for her). I'm going out to buy vodka now, and maybe a short, tight-fitting "fashionable" skirt (especially since I know his wife doesn't wear that kind of skirt). It is a lovely hell, but hell nonetheless. I wonder if he, too, since Tuesday, has been afraid of what is happening between us.

Sunday 20

A call last night at half past seven. Immediately there's a complete about-face, as usual. A kind of tranquility sets in, a calm happiness, and then the waiting begins for the next meeting—desire, the planning of caresses. Naturally, I have very little urge to work (the piece on the Revolution).

Tuesday 22

Tonight, a party at Irène's. He'll be there with his wife. Ordeal. Especially since we won't be able to be alone together later. Such obstacles heighten desire—their sole appeal, as far as I can see. Last night, he calls me, obviously drunk, already (so this is becoming a frequent occurrence? I hadn't noticed it in Moscow), and groping for words. Twenty minutes later, he calls back and starts with "me too," as if responding to something I said during the previous call, perhaps an "I love you." He is muddled, laughs too much. But he says "I love you" at the end, though only after I had said it. I am very much in love, it's a beautiful story.

Evening: difficult, indeed. I looked for the source of the pain, the infinite sadness I felt on returning from the evening at Irène's. It isn't jealousy. Maria, S's wife, is not very attractive—definitely "sturdy," as people say of fabric, with nothing else going for her. The sadness has to do with knowing, through unconscious memory, some of what she might be suffering. I "was" her, in the old days, at parties where my husband showed interest in other women and G, his mistress, was present. Several times, S fixes me with an intense gaze. So I suddenly decide to talk to his wife. We "converse" at length, S, his wife, and others such as Marie R and Alain N. Acting so congenial, when we're really two-faced bastards. Which explains my sadness. That and the fact of having to wait until Thursday to be alone with him.

She wore a long, shapeless skirt with flesh-colored tights, and me a very short skirt with black stockings. One could not imagine two women more different in terms of height, hair and eye color, body (she's a little dumpy) and clothing. The mother and the whore.

Wednesday 23

It is difficult now to forget that presence next to S (the couple: that word, that thing I abhor). At the same time, it painfully increases desire. I am, for as long as it lasts, the preferred one, the true object of desire. I understand Tristan and Isolde, the passion that consumes and cannot be extinguished, despite—because of—the obstacles.

Thursday 24

Fog, gray and gloomy weather. Today, I'm afraid he's bored and that we won't even last through Christmas. Besides, this life divvied up by phone calls, and meetings that are, all in all, quite rare, once a week (it was twice, in October), is stupid and empty. I mean "empty" in relation to the outside world (nothing really interests me anymore), but full in terms of feeling.

Today's disappointments:

1) he still hasn't said the tender things I've been waiting for

2) after the France-USSR association event, he left with the girls from the embassy without driving me back to Cergy.

And I realize that my article on the Revolution is appallingly bad. Sleep, yes.

And I'm already wondering (but with revulsion) "when will he call?"

Friday 25

Two amusing examples of behavior: I light candles in churches for success in love, and this afternoon I went to the "Sex" section of the book department at the Printemps. I leaf through the pages, people come and go: a man who is browsing too, a woman who brushes against me so I think might be a lesbian. Then to the cash desk, with *Treatise on Caresses* by Dr. Leleu and *The Couple and Love: Techniques of Lovemaking*, 75 photographs, 800,000 copies sold. Women stand in line behind me. I remain poker-faced. The clerk wraps the books up. I do not pay with my bank card, so no one will know my name, and I won't read these books on the RER. I buy them for the perfection, the sublimation of the flesh.

Sunday 27

Is this a life? Yes, it is probably better than a vacuum. I wait by the phone for the call that may not come. I do not open the books on "techniques of lovemaking," afraid to fall into the torture of desire without certainty of when we can be together, like the people in the books . . . Admit it: I've never wanted anything but love. And literature. I only wrote to fill the void, to give myself a way to tell and endure the memory of '58, the abortion, the parents' love—everything that was a story of flesh and love. If he doesn't call by tomorrow evening, that is, four days after our last meeting, I think I'll have to start imagining the end, and, if possible, make it come more quickly.

This week, remember: coming into possession of his big new car will certainly occupy him more than any thought of me.

Monday 28

7:30 p.m. Perhaps what most keeps me attached to S is my failure to understand his behavior. Also my difficulty in deciphering his cultural codes, and even situating him socially, intellectually, which in the case of a French man is quite easy to do.

An excruciating wait. Feverishly I correct essays to keep myself busy, waiting for the call, the voice that instantly tells me I exist and am desired. Why am I sure each time that it's over and he won't call again, because of what old fear?

8:45 p.m. The call. Each time, it is "destiny," a sign from the beyond—terror, instantaneous joy. When I answer, the excruciating fear that it's a mistake, a false sign from that same destiny. It's him, for tomorrow, four o'clock. Devastating joy, the immediate erasure of an anguish that was at its peak this evening . . . I no longer want to correct those essays that I threw myself upon, in order to forget. I want to cry, or laugh. I'm going to wash the floors, the loo, create a little cleanliness to welcome him, the "male," the man, he whom I recognize as a god, for a while, before disillusionment, oblivion.

Tuesday 29

11:00 p.m. At around four o'clock, waiting for him, I felt a very deep fear. Of seeing him again, and therefore adding an afternoon which, by dint of accumulation, will surely lead us to the point of saturation and the absence of desire. I never reason in terms of attachment that increases as we get to know each other, but in terms of decline and disillusionment.

We made love the way we did one evening in Leningrad. Beautiful. Then in the vestibule, the way we did two weeks ago. Beautiful, again. But already it's "the way we did." He was wearing underpants that were obviously Russian: white, the elastic too wide and coming a little unstitched. (My father had the same ones!)

I'm tired, and quite sad, probably because I expect too much from this affair, after expecting nothing whatsoever from it (in Leningrad).

"I don't want us to break up!" he said. Yes, of course, but then he says: "I make love with my wife, sometimes—often." Immediately I think, "These words will etch themselves upon me and come back in force." But they don't, or not as much as I feared, in the end. Is he lying when he says he's never had a French girlfriend? I sense that he doesn't often cheat on his wife. Maybe I'm the first in a long time. After all, he comes to Cergy from Paris a little more than once a week and stays the whole evening. I may be underestimating his attachment. But now he only calls four days after our last meeting.

December
Saturday 3

More than two months already. I walked past Brummell this evening, at the corner of rue du Havre and rue de Provence. A harrowing beggar, mouth hanging open, holds out some kind of blue wool cap. I retrace my steps and give him ten francs, wishing for S to call me this evening. Four days . . .

10:00 p.m. Why are the signs always there, ironic and astounding? He just called. I think of the beggar, tall, terrible, and full of pain, like Christ, of giving him money, of the phone call this evening. We'll see each other Thursday. I think of all the things I need to do before then—lunch with Antoine Gallimard, a trip to Luxembourg, especially—and feel exhausted.

Anyway, what does this sign really mean, the phone call from the Latin Quarter? That he's thinking of me? But in what way? There's nothing more impossible to imagine than the desire, the emotion, of the Other. And yet, only that is beautiful. All I dream of is this perfection, without yet being sure of attaining it—of being the "last woman," the one who erases all the others, with her attentiveness, her skilled knowledge of his body: the "sublime affair."

Today, I could not see S because of the lunch with Antoine Gallimard and Pascal Quignard (and I had my period). Am sick at heart because I'm going to Luxembourg, with loathing, for two days. Signs don't always pan out. Today, I gave money to a beggar at the Gare Saint-Lazare, making a wish for S to call, and later to the punk with all the earrings who got on the train stopped in the station. And then to that singer! We live in a world of mendicancy to which we've grown accustomed, almost esthetic. It's part of the city, the scenery in the station, the tower blocks beyond the tracks with brand names in gigantic letters—"Varta," "Salec"—high on their sun-lit facades. There was that commercial a few months ago, "Welcome to a world of challenge, the world of Rhône-Poulenc.*" You can't be serious.

It's been over a week since S has come around. Too long. I review my life since then, and am amazed by how many stupid, unpleasant events there have been: the meal with H, the young people's book award in Montreuil, the last of my courses on Robbe-Grillet, and the lunch today. That life consists of this accumulation of endeavors, bland and burdensome actions, punctuated only occasionally by moments of intensity, outside of time, is horrifying. Love and writing are the only two things in the world that I can bear, the rest is darkness. Tonight I have neither.

---

* Rhône-Poulenc, a French chemical and pharmaceutical company founded in 1928 which no longer exists under this name.

Thursday 8

I'm afraid he won't be able to come tomorrow because of the earthquake in Armenia. The embassy personnel are run off their feet. Ten very long days, and now maybe nothing. So much longing again this morning, on the train, and then, closer to the time of his arrival, I'm almost frozen with anxiety, the fear of "less"—less happiness, less desire to be together than before.

Friday 9

10:25 a.m. Is that his car?

Fear that he will not come and not let me know ahead of time. Fear, too, that he's already here. Fear of the moment when I hear the car brake—that sound. Fear of not being beautiful enough, and especially of not giving him enough pleasure. But if I didn't have all these fears, it would mean I was indifferent.

6:10 p.m. He left at five past five. Barely two and a half hours together. I want to think that the signs of decline were obvious, this time. But he missed Sakharov's talk at the embassy in order to come to Cergy. Lovemaking was very good the first time, but I didn't think so the second time. Is he faking? He's elusive even in his sexual behavior. I don't know anything about him. This Russian world will remain forever unknown to me—the world of diplomacy, the Soviet apparatus . . . It's obvious that I've always invested too much imagination in men. I get lost, my self dissolves. I don't know what binds him to me, if it's just my name, the fact that I'm a writer—it makes me want to run away. The greatest fear is that he has another woman. He was drawn to the title of a book in Spanish, something like "in the arms of the mature woman (*madura*)." That's me, of course. And how can I know for sure that certain things do not upset him, such as my inviting Makanine [a Russian writer] to dinner, or the phone call I received from SA when he was with me?

How to interpret his interest in the title, "in the arms of the mature woman" (he says "matured")? As both fear and recognition of his desire for this kind of woman?

"Are you going away over Christmas?" Does he mean "It would be better if you left, then I wouldn't have to come see you," or "It would be nice if you stayed around"?

It may also be that these phrases have no importance for him, but are just the sort of thing that people say . . .

Likewise, his not attending Sakharov's conference may have been deliberate, political: Sakharov is a dissident, while he is "a loyalist."

I reread what I wrote last Saturday. Six days, usually nothing, are now an eternity. Passion fills life to bursting.

Sunday 11

Gray day. Reminds me of December '63, when I was pregnant and wanted an abortion: the university residence, the state of complete and utter dereliction, my desire to sleep in the afternoon (ditto at P's, in '84). This kind of sleep (more a huge weariness with life) is comparable to that of drunks on benches in the subway. I will probably never spend a whole night with S. I could have done so just one time, in Leningrad, and I didn't want to then. In '85 too, the same gray weather, the same melancholy, same dissatisfaction. Right now, I suffer from not writing. Student essays, lessons, emotional life, outings, receptions—it's all a vacuum. I no longer seek truth since I no longer write, the two are intertwined. I'm also very sexual, there's no other word for it: being admired, etc. are not what matters to me. What matters is having and giving pleasure—desire, real eroticism, not the imaginary kind, as in porn on TV or in movies.

Evening. I reread the end of the other notebook, and the whole story with S flashes through my mind. I see how much time has already passed, and I weep. Only beginnings are truly beautiful. Yet in the garden of Sceaux, as at the studio, in October, it was nothing special. So why weep?

I don't want him to come to my Soviet dinner on Tuesday. It would be too difficult with him there. I love him (= I need him), and I'm not sure he loves me. Same old story.

Tuesday 13

He did not come to my dinner, and it was probably much better that way. I'm not sure that having people here was a good idea. It's over now. I think I hate to entertain. I live in perpetual anxiety that everything's a failure (halfway true, tonight). My skirt is stained and there's a mountain of dishes to put away. I have a mad desire to see S as soon as possible, as if the presence of the others had deepened the lack of him inside me.

Wednesday 14

He was supposed to call today. For the first time, he didn't (however, I was out from 4:00 to 8:00 p.m.). The countdown may already have begun. Everything's so black that I want to stay home. The outside world fills me with horror. Here alone, in this house, it's less unbearable. And there's the phone, therefore hope. When I'm out, there's no escape, I'm a woman on the verge of tears. Tatyana Tolstaya and her "eternal things," her way of saying, like Nathalie Sarraute, "I am a writer and I am a citizen, the two do not intrude on each other . . ." But all I've really retained of her are the "Russian" gestures, shaking the hand in front of the face in negation/derision, and an indefinable facial expression that S sometimes has. I don't like the way she speaks of her country with derision: "The USSR is a real gift for a writer" (because it's so terrible).

Thursday 15

Silence, still. I feel so low that I try to remember similar times: '58 and '63 return, inexorably. I know that all it would take is a call (that word is so very apt) to make me want to live again. If one day people read this journal, they'll see that there was indeed "alienation in the work of Annie Ernaux," and not only in the work but even more so in her life. My relationships with men follow this invincible course:

a) initial indifference, even disgust

b) "illumination," more or less physical

c) happy relations, fairly controlled, and even spells of boredom

d) suffering, infinite lack.

And then comes the time (I'm there now) when the pain is so all-consuming that moments of happiness are nothing more than future pain; they increase the pain.

e) The last step is separation, before arriving at the most perfect stage of all: indifference.

8:45 p.m. It's very hard—much more, I think, than with P, four years ago, in the summer. It is clear that if he doesn't call me tonight (when he was supposed to call me *yesterday*), it's over, for reasons unknown to me (of course, that's exactly what you never do know, or only find out later). To get through this evening without too many tears is all I ask. Writing doesn't make you suffer in the same way, though it's just as hard. What I feel now is a wrenching sensation, a sense of exclusion, the desire for death. At eighteen, I ate to compensate. At forty-eight, I know there is no possible compensation. I imagine a book that would begin with "I loved a man" or even "I still love a man." When I think of him, I see him naked in my bedroom. I undress him, I think only of his erect penis, his desire. That is how I should tell it.

9:45 p.m. He did call, and I'm no happier for it (which means the cycle of pain has begun). We see each other Tuesday, so five days from now. Which means that he doesn't need to see me more often. That he may have someone else, despite his preposterous underpants. That I'm an honorary woman, to be honored more and more remotely, but not let go—anything but that! I know the routine. Still, I wait. Better than nothing?

Friday 16

Black mornings: a day simply to be got through, nothing more. It is still night. There are hundreds and hundreds of mornings like this, behind and ahead of me. I masturbate while thinking of S, which makes it worse. Well, not quite.

Tuesday 20

He never lets me know by phone, ahead of time, when exactly he'll arrive. Since Thursday evening, when the date was set, I could have died or fallen ill. No way of notifying him. The shadow lover. And there's always the fear, even terror (I have the runs each time) of seeing him again, whereas for the entire night, all I felt was desire, all-consuming desire. The car arriving . . . Each time, it's as if I am going to lose my virginity all over again.

10:40 a.m. What if he doesn't come?
Or if the decline that has begun were to continue? The weather is splendid, as it was in November. It's not November anymore, however

3:30 p.m. He arrived just as I finished writing "however." Did the good weather bring him? A blissful encounter. He brings gifts and promises me a photo. And it occurs to me that he loves me a little, in his own way, an extra-marital kind of way, like ticking a box, though maybe not as much as I think. His attachment is sensual too, a little wild. The impossibility of knowing what I mean to him, much greater than it was with P, is, at the same time, very exciting. He was driving his "fancy car," something that—yes—he has in common with my ex-husband, socially. How tired I am. How happy it makes me to make him come, to make him happy. "What are you doing?" he says in his Russian accent when he is aroused, as I caress him with my mouth. Unforgettable. In other words, I don't stand a chance, it's the road to perdition, I spend my energy, my life, as if there were no tomorrow.

Wednesday 21

Hard to say what he will think of my gift, really the kind of gift an old mistress gives a gigolo, considering the price. Today, I gave ten francs to the dreadful apparition in the Opéra metro station: the woman with the twisted, half-formed hands and feet, who has been sitting doubled-over against the wall for the past year, at least. I check for signs. But why would he call me, when he was here only yesterday. That was his tick in the box. So much for the desires I project onto the beggars I've assigned to intercede on my behalf with fate! Reality prevails over imagination.

Thursday 22

Tonight, I had a kind of revelation about the lavishness of my gift to a man who may just see me as a piece of ass only slightly more rewarding than another (but here I'm painting a picture that is exaggeratedly bleak). The whole problem remains, as ever, what do I mean to him? "What is Hecuba to him, or he to Hecuba?" [*Hamlet*]

Evening. What if he wants to break up? The fact that he told me the opposite on November 29 (a month ago—an eternity . . .) signifies nothing. Tonight, I consider the possibility that he won't come at all next week. If that's the case, I must have the courage to face facts and break up with him, but do it with class by giving him his present.

Every night is black and I'm too dependent, at the mercy of the phone. He's supposed to call, at the latest (that is, according to past standards), on Saturday or Sunday evening. If it goes beyond, a decision must be made.

Saturday 24

A morning as black as that day before Easter or Quasimodo Sunday, 1986. This is by far the most alienating relationship I've had since the one with Philippe twenty-five years ago. I write in this notebook tirelessly, as I wrote about my mother when she was in hospital, near the end. If only it could at least *serve a purpose*. Last night, I was sure he'd had enough of me and wouldn't call until January. This morning I still feel a little that way.

At one o'clock, the chilly greeting card arrives, which I view as a sign: "best wishes," with his signature. On second thought, it doesn't mean anything, it's just a necessarily official card. Seen in another way, as a sign of breakup (a line of thinking in which I've been immersed for two weeks), it portends the cordial relations coming to replace the ones that preceded them.

Sunday 25

From eight to ten o'clock, utter darkness: he doesn't call and I wait, end of story. And at this moment, contrary to Proust, I do not believe it would take very little, just a tiny movement of the will, to pass through suffering, break through this paper hoop and beyond that point be free.

Monday 26

To have changed so little, waited, at age sixteen (in January and February), for a sign of life from G de V, at eighteen for a sign from CG (the worst time of all), at twenty-three for Ph, in Rome, and a few years ago for P. This time I've exceeded by one day the deadline I set myself. But a call tonight would still be acceptable because of the hole of the Christmas holiday. After that . . .

To change so little, right down to the desire for pregnancy. But I haven't yet taken measures to make this outcome possible (however, I don't think I'll take the pill this month).

It takes little *self-confidence* on my part to be capable of all this folly!

10:45 p.m. He called but doesn't know when he will come. "I'll try to see you this week." "I'll try," that awful phrase for when you don't feel like doing something. I just need a little calm, a little balm for my pain.

Tuesday 27

Of course (and yet I waited . . .), he did not call as expected, "tomorrow, or the day after." I'm on the verge of tears and nausea. And never alone, what's more, Éric's always here, on the alert for the days when S will come around, and probably happy that he doesn't. I don't know what to think—or rather I do. I am perfectly indifferent to S, but tonight I am grappling with several tons of non-being and disgust. To sleep . . . to sleep . . .

Wednesday 28

I didn't really sleep, overwhelmed by horror: tears, and the certainty of having been quietly dumped. Dreams of my ex-husband trying to fuck me, which I found excruciating, haunted by S. "Where life closes around us, intelligence pierces a way out," says Proust. At night, there is no intelligence, only life in its magma of contradictions and suffering, with no way out. The paper hoop was a concrete slab. I don't think I've had a night like this in six years, not since my separation from Philippe. Again, I've reached the point of wanting a clean break. Three months.

I don't wonder at my madness in '58, after CG, my two years of bulimia, my distress *because of men*. I know very well it's *that* which makes me write, the lack of fulfillment in love, a bottomless pit.

There is a time in a love affair when you run—everything still lies ahead, full of hope—and another time when everything tumbles into the past and what lies ahead will never be anything but repetition and decline. I situate the moment it changed as sometime in November, but cannot be more precise. More likely December, when I invited Makanine to dinner. October and November were two very beautiful months—sunny, moreover—and December very dark. Why write this, if not to force the future to be sunny again? It's rarely with the same man.

I slept for an hour this afternoon, in the bedroom (generally a sign of great dereliction). I almost broke one of the bedside lamps as I was waking up.

I am a voracious woman—really, that is the only fairly accurate thing that can be said of me.

Thursday 29

10:30 p.m. I'd turned off the light. Three times, the phone rings once, and there's no one on the line. Ten minutes later: "Friday, ten o'clock." For the first time in my life, I *weep* for joy. And then I know that nothing can be worse for me than this, to be caught up in this vicious cycle—as with Philippe in Rome, but with no official outcome. Which is fortunate, because naturally I would fall into the trap of marriage, etc.

Friday 30

I'm in a hole. Still at the stage when he's not quite gone and I'm still certain that he likes to be with me. Worrying about my gift—too lavish. A memory of sweetness: "What is the meaning of those flowers?" he asked of the primroses next to my bed.

Obvious jealousy, since I taught him that in France, flowers have meaning. The proof always lies in jealousy. I set him straight and offer him some other primroses from the garden.

Today, he kneels down before my sex, as I do with him. Wonderful undressing of each other and ourselves. Yes he's beautiful, "my heart-throb," as DL calls him (without knowing who he is)—DL with his blasé "seen it all" Parisian mentality that I despise.

On TV, I heard this Aznavour song which I'd forgotten, *Vivre, je veux vivre avec toi*, "Live, I want to live with you." I'm sixteen, still sixteen, swept away by the memory of that time and that crazy love. With S, it's as if all the unfinished or imperfect loves of my youth were fulfilled: G de V, Pierre D, all those who disappointed me, and who, I know now, could not have done otherwise. They were no worse than others. Now I know I cannot "live with you." It has to remain a dream, a sorrow.

This afternoon, I'm overwhelmed by the idea that I'm like Anna Karenina. Anna, mad about Vronski. Fear.

Saturday 31

Tonight, F. Mitterrand's New Year's address: his speech is on the Left, in spite of it all. At the end, for the first time, *La Marseillaise* is sung. I have a little shiver down my back, which for me is the sign of absolute emotion. *La Marseillaise*! My father sang it to me, it's the end of the war, the song of freedom. '89! For me it has special meaning, I'm on the side of revolution and always have been. *Entendez-vous dans nos (les?) campagnes / Mugir(!) ces féroces soldats? / Ils viennent jusque dans nos bras /*

Éngorger *nos fils, nos compagnes / Aux armes, citoyens . . .** So windy, so overblown, but the words aren't important, only the music is, and that rallying cry, *Aux armes, citoyens.*

1988: a satisfactory year, in the main, but too much media ferment. Strictly speaking, I accomplished nothing. The best moments: Venice, the USSR, and of course, the "story" I've been involved in since the end of September, the twenty-fifth to be exact, the day the clocks changed to wintertime. We had an autumn together—what other season(s) will there be?

To state the obvious: objectively, when you go to bed with someone, the things you do are the same, whether or not you're in love.

1989

January
Sunday 1

I am alone, absolutely, on this January 1. This has not happened to me for a long time. In '64, I returned to the university residence from Vernon and spent the day alone in my eight square meters. But this afternoon, Éric and his girlfriend will be here. Anyway, I feel no sadness about it. A dream from last night: I'm walking along the edge of a field with a scythe while

---

* Do you hear, in our countrysides / The roar of those fearsome soldiers / Coming right into our arms / To cut the throats of our sons and our women? / To arms, oh citizens . . .

young men work. They ask me for the scythe, I don't want to give it to them. This is the field in Yvetot where I fell in love for the first time, at thirteen. Someone, an old laborer, says that he earns 20,000 francs per month and I think to myself that manual labor is well paid, compared to teaching. Then Éric appears (because of my fears for his future?), and a bishop whom people have been expecting arrives, and with no shyness I join in on what happens next. Hard to interpret, except maybe for the scythe: fear of aging. But this isn't yet the year when I enter my fifties.

I may write to S, as I often do—he gets the letter when he comes here, I'm forbidden to send him things by mail, as I am to phone him! the stuff of a novel—but I know I might as well be writing to a wall. There is *never* any *visible* reaction to what I write him, except when I give an order ("next time, come straight in, without knocking," etc.), and he obeys. What is the meaning of his desire to make love in the dark, right from the beginning, Leningrad? He also closes his eyes, always. Except when I caress his sex with my mouth and he raises himself to watch. If I look up, he immediately looks away. Is this from shame, repression?

Tuesday 3

This morning's drama: he'll call tonight, or tomorrow, and say it's over. Right now this seems so plausible that my heart is in my throat. He'll have every possible reason: the spark has gone out—it's too difficult to see each other again—he's afraid I'm too clingy (for example, he feels awkward about the overly lavish gift). I am thinking all this because in the letter I gave him last time, I asked him to tell me what he really wants. He can "seize the opportunity," as in the story of Madame de La Pommeraye in *Jacques le Fataliste*.

My whole life has been an effort to tear myself away from male desire, in other words, from my own desire. In '63, I repeated to myself these words from the Bible: "And I will extend peace to her like a river," not even knowing that these words referred to my desire, sperm flowing over me like a river.

Wednesday 4

This evening, it's still over. He's not going to call. I try to hold on, not hit bottom like last Tuesday. But it's horrific, for I always see my presentiments come true, the boredom I've sensed since the end of November having become so visible that I must be completely out of my mind to still believe he's attached to me. Scornfully I think: I'm like that girl who for the last six months has written me love letters that I don't even read. I too write love letters to someone who doesn't love me. But why love? He promised nothing, and all I ask for is beauty. There is no more beauty because there is no more anything.

Thursday 5

4:10 p.m. He called this morning. He's coming in a few minutes. It's always the same insane panic, the waiting without a thought in my head. It occurred to me, driving home from a hasty trip to the shops, that I could have run into another car and wouldn't have stopped, wouldn't have felt any guilt. So where does guilt come from, a life too empty, lacking in desire? Which is truer, desire or guilt?

5:00 p.m. He's not here. I tell myself he won't be coming now. I took the phone off the hook around four so we wouldn't be disturbed. Maybe he's tried calling to let me know.

10:30 p.m. I didn't hear him arrive. He entered quietly. So then everything I imagined was untrue? He wants me, is happy to see me, we make love divinely. But again this time, he'd had a lot to drink, whiskey late in the evening. He cried out with pleasure for the first time (well, he moaned very loudly). When we're together, when we're making love, I'm sure he has no one else, and cares about me. Very much. Then, days go by and I'm sure it's all over. I'm the same way with exams, which I feel less and less likely to have passed and more and more miserably failed the more time goes by since the day I took them.

I will leave this state of fatigue, from which I'd like never to emerge: no thoughts, just the memory of caresses, and his body— in the bathroom (anal sex, which he asked for expressly), in the bedroom and again the bathroom. He gets dressed, it takes a very long time (he's really had a lot to drink). He lists the brands of all his clothes—Rodier, Pierre Cardin (the belt that I undo so easily!)—even that of his shoes. So wonderfully parvenu, like me, but from the other side of Europe. He's very proud of his Dupont lighter, contrary to what I'd imagined, though I should have foreseen it, and anyway I must have known it, otherwise I wouldn't have given it to him. Will his wife believe the lie he told her?

He does not know how to unfasten garters.

Friday 6

I understand this desire to shower gifts on a person we love to demonstrate possession (Proust, *La prisonnière*), while knowing that it does nothing to bind him to us, but only makes him proud (of arousing so much love) and heightens his narcissism. This works against the giver, who is short on narcissism. Well, anyway, I love him with all my emptiness.

Sunday 8

How can desire be reborn and become this obsession? Spending an entire night with him is my only goal in life now, and I wonder what I would not willingly sacrifice in order to have it. I'm sick to death of that paper for the London conference.

I have not yet been able to decide between two visions of S, the young and handsome womanizer, with an intellectually superior, slightly jealous wife (= my husband and me), or the shy young man who is anxious not to hurt his wife and so has not had many affairs. His attitude in love—a certain lack of experience—leads me to believe that the second is the truer. But I'll never know, except through outside witnesses, who are more difficult to find here than elsewhere (the Russian milieu).

Monday 9

So much waiting, and the feeling he won't find time to come this week (the president of the VAAP is arriving). I write these details to remember, to lock them in, but maybe that's not all:

I've always talked about myself *to* someone, right from the start. The best I can hope for is a call from him on Wednesday (six days from now).

My first novel was initially entitled *L'arbre*—the tree: an obvious phallic symbol, and also a reference to a song by Dario Moreno that I loved in '58, "Histoire d'un amour": *Un grand arbre qui se dresse / Plein de force et de tendresse / Vers le jour qui va venir.** Only I can elucidate my life, not the critics. The tree—an obsession.

The doubts begin again, the feeling that he has other women. Another thing: I don't give a damn about AIDS with him. In any case, other men don't exist for me right now. And I'm not taking the pill—to relive the catastrophe, death in my belly, as in '64? But at forty-eight, I'm unlikely to get pregnant.

I wait for him with many scenarios in mind (where and how to make love, etc.), without really knowing if he will come. This chasm—between imagination, desire and reality—is unbearable.

Tuesday 10

10:00 p.m. There's little hope of his calling tonight. Heard "Cécile, ma fille," by Nougaro, the song I listened to when I was pregnant with Éric: twenty-four years ago. I am sickened by time, by the image of that vanished self, though I care nothing for her because I prefer myself now. But that self is contained

---

* A great tree that stretches its branches, / Full of strength and tenderness, / Toward the breaking day.

in the present one, along with the others, like millions of Russian dolls. A wino insulted me at the hardware store, which he entered to ask for methylated spirits (to drink): "Slut! Whore!" He ranted on and on, in a frenzy, willing me to die "boiled alive with my throat cut." An unpleasant feeling. Whore . . .

Naturally, I will not go to the *L'Événement du jeudi* cocktail party tomorrow because he could call while I'm out . . . *

11:00 p.m. He called and may be able to come around. He doesn't know when . . . That voice: deep, even deeper tonight, with his Russian intonations, his slow, expansive *yes*es. I'll go to the co(c)ktail (clearly, I don't know how to write this word, which I have not often come across) because he called.

Thursday 12

I'd have done better to work on my paper for the Barbican instead of going to the cocktail party. Abysmal. Parisian. More journalists than writers (and always the same writers—Sollers, Bianciotti, etc.). Dreamt last night of a church that I want to enter. But the crypt can only be reached by climbing a rope ladder, impossible for me. The nave and the chancel are being repaired and I go in, after a moment's hesitation. There's a chimpanzee, which then reveals itself to be a bear, at the altar. I go out again. It follows me and grows more and more affectionate, but I find it threatening. In spite of my pleas, no one helps me to chase it away. Finally, I succeed. It seems that the bear is a symbol of Russia, but I was unaware of this. The dream

---

* *L'Événement du jeudi* was a French weekly publication that was created in 1984 and folded in 2001.

is connected to S, who met bears in Siberia when he worked on the log drives. S is like a fair-haired version of Guy D (who is also tall with deep-set eyes though his are blue-green), with the mouth of Luis F. I have to work and am tormented by waiting. The disappointment of possibly not seeing him in the next two days devastates me.

6:00 p.m. The text for the conference is abhorrent to me because there's less and less hope that S will come tomorrow. I work with no prospect of a reward—so, for nothing. Explaining the mechanics of the struggle between cultures is exhausting in the extreme and the "glory" it will bring does not hold a candle to an hour spent with S. It's been more than a week since we've seen each other. I have no future, other than the date of our next meeting. And when none has been arranged, there is absolutely no future.

Friday 13

If, as they say in the horoscopes, Venus is in my sign, you'd never guess it. Dreamt I had a child, I held him in my arms and showed him to all the physiotherapists at the Clinique la Châtaigneraie. Then I left him on a table for a few seconds. A shriek. I discover that his neck is broken and he is smaller than a hand. I know that he will die. I am weeping as I write this. I know I am "reliving" my abortion, the unbearable again.

9:00 a.m. At what time will I have to break through the hoop of pain and finish the text for this nightmare lecture? At ten o'clock, definitely—in other words, when there's no longer any possibility of his calling to say he'll come today.

3:30 p.m. I didn't know it would be *so hard* to live with this dead-end affair. I recopy the text for this (dreadful) lecture. I don't know when I'll see him again, but it is *now, today,* that I'd like to see him, and my desire for him is frightening, reduces me to tears. Why did he give me hope on Tuesday? A first lie.

I understand people not wanting to go on living, sometimes. Today is "Friday the 13th," as in the film. Next, two days in London—in other words, no possibility of a phone call. Basically, the *hard* part is not that he is going back to Moscow but that he's still in Paris.

Monday 16

London. Yesterday I returned to 21 Kenver Avenue. First, the Tube at Tottenham Court Road. The seats are still covered in fabric, but everything is dirty and run-down. I got off at East Finchley, by the bridge over the High Road, which I'd forgotten. I took the bus, asking for the stop for Granville Road, as in the past. The driver doesn't know which one it is, but stops there nonetheless. To the right, I see the swimming pool, which I've also forgotten. The Portners' house has been transformed, apparently made more practical—the entrance is a kitchen. Something like a "downgrading" of the house and also the street, which seems to me less residential and less chic than before (I had just arrived from Yvetot, don't forget). But all that whiteness, uniformity, boredom—how horrible it must have been, indescribable. Then the church: Christchurch, exactly the same, with the bench in front. No shops I recognize, except for the Woolworth's. No more movie theater, no tobacconist's (it was called "Rabbit"), no little café where the youth of 1960 gathered round the jukebox and that bespectacled woman washed cups amid the noise and exclamations. She lives only in my book of '62–'63, which is unpublished.* Except for the shape of the street, the High Road, a pub that's been turned into a steakhouse, everything was different, especially the shops. They are the least stable element, the form most sensitive to change (so the economy prevails over all, still?). I took the tube back to Woodside Park, and in the street that had changed so little, wondered whether it was in the adjoining park that I started to write my first book, in August 1960, "Horses danced by the sea." What came next was a girl getting up from a bed where she'd been lying with a guy (always the same story, the only one). Those slow-moving horses, mired in their dance, expressed the feeling of heaviness after love. As I remember well . . .

Yesterday's walk was unreal. The only permanent reality is the images I retain of 1960–61, some of which are contained in *The Five O'Clock Sun*** ("Blood at five bells," my ex-husband called it). All the conference participants made a beeline for the museums while I plunged back into my past life in North Finchley. I'm not a culture hound. The only thing that matters to me is to seize life and time, understand, and take pleasure.

It will be six days since the last time S called, and twelve since

---

* *L'arbre*, a short work the author submitted to Le Seuil and later, under the title *Du soleil à cinq heures* (The Five O'Clock Sun), to Buchet-Chastel. Both publishers rejected it.
** Ibid.

we last saw each other. During my two days away, he does not seem to have called. Back here, in this place where he comes to see me, the torture begins anew.

Tuesday 17

10:20 a.m. He is going to come. During the night, I thought, the only happy time in this affair is the night before we meet. (Who wrote "la nuit qui précéda sa mort fut la plus belle de sa vie"? Apollinaire? [Éluard].)* I don't understand this desire I have for S, the panic when I hear his car, that feeling of being wonderfully lost.

2:30 p.m. He was more preoccupied, as if tired, but still full of desire. Impenetrable: why did he leave so abruptly, closing the door behind him? Was it due to haste or emotion about leaving? No tender words, and yet what passionate tenderness in his gestures. (He now knows how to unfasten garters. I'm writing this down because that's the detail that will matter to me most later.) Love twice in two hours, as usual. And he is going away for a week and coming back when I leave for West Germany.

I reread these two paragraphs in succession—same handwriting, no break, the same black stream of spidery scrawl. Between the two was a time when nothing mattered but the Other—only him, only skin, the abyss of desire. How could writing convey this? It will always fall short. And yet it's all I have when he's not here.

---

* The lines by Éluard read: *La nuit qui précéda sa mort / fut la plus courte de sa vie* (The night before his death / Was the shortest of his life).

Thursday 19

At the Globe bookstore, people are speaking Russian, and all at once I know I've imagined it all, and that S and I are light years apart, and it was just a meeting in Leningrad, a meeting of bodies. But no, this desire is reality. I won't see him again until the end of January. Maybe the thirty-first?

Thought maybe I should take advantage of this time to try to forget him. I have some kind of cystitis, as in October–November, very painful (connected to him, of course).

Sunday 22

Evening. Another useless afternoon. In the RER, a guy stares at me, etc. Honestly, what's the attraction? No sign of S. He has no interest in phoning, since he cannot come over and fuck. "Keeping in touch" is a concept unknown to him. Vronski—and how! A Vronski raised in Marxism-Leninism, the Komsomol, a Party member, perfectly pragmatic. But I cannot think of his smooth body, his white skin, his face, without tears of desire.

This morning, at the Auber station, on the Balard side, a man sat, head in hands, on the stairs. All you could see was gray hair. In front of him, a jar lid with ten and twenty centime coins in it. I give him ten francs, wishing very hard for S to call me from the South. At this moment, he must be at the home of André S. But what power do wishes have over "it," the situation over which I have no control? Not for all the alms in the world . . .

Monday 23

Dreamed of my mother's coffin, which I want to cover with flowers (a poor summary of the dream: the extreme difficulty of *relating* dreams, they always resist the telling—only real writing could properly convey them). She has just died, and I know that one day I'll be in her place.

This journal should have two columns, one for immediate writing, the other for interpretation a few weeks later. That would be a wide column because I could write several interpretations.

Tuesday 24

I cannot reread this journal without pain (the last pages). What if S is making use of what I told him about breaking up with P when he was away in New York, and doing the same with me? His hasty departure the other night would, in that case, have indicated the twinge of emotion a person can feel when leaving someone they'll never see again, even if their mind is made up. I'm afraid that my return from West Germany and the Russian-American women writers' days will be grueling. If he doesn't call on Saturday night, it will be a very bad sign. Again I have this strange, painful false-cystitis, which does not help matters any.

Thursday 26

This room in Hanover, blue, across from the Neue Rathaus, reminds me of the room in Lille in '85. A background noise of cars. Like in Rome, too. What a strange impression. Of solitude, of being nowhere. All these rooms nestled inside each other.

Saturday 28

Back from Germany. I felt no pain when I was there. As I got closer to Paris, the waiting and desire returned. Yet it's as if I've already accepted that, for example, he won't call tonight. Tomorrow, to my great dismay, he may be at Irène's. Dismay, because of all those women writers, of whom I am, of course, jealous. Régine Deforges, Rihoit, Annie Cohen-Solal. Quite pretty women, on the French side. On the Russian side, chubby or elderly, as usual. As for the Americans, hard to say.

The sudden odor of the house in Boisgibault, in a Hanover church, the Marketkirche. At the Pinacothek, in Munich, a Millet country scene: a mother in a doorway getting a little half-naked boy ready to pee, a little girl watching intently. A scene from my childhood (well not quite, but the curiosity is the same)—also a scene from when I was thirteen: seeing my aunt through the small dormer window, getting a little boy ready to pee while a little girl watched, maybe my cousin Francette (that gesture used by women to lift a little boy's penis; the intense curiosity of little girls). In the Millet, it is all strikingly true to life, but flat.

Some very over-the-top paintings by someone called von Kaug. In a huge Last Judgment, a man bound for hell claws at his chest and we see the bloody trails of his fingernails on his skin.

Has he forgotten me? (What a lame expression! No, strictly

speaking, obviously he hasn't forgotten me. He no longer needs me: much more accurate.)

Sunday 29

2:30 p.m. The prospect of going to Irène's, without knowing if he'll be there (if he doesn't call, there's a greater and greater chance that he will be), of seeing him without knowing what new feelings he may have about me. And all in front of these women who, of course, hate each other. Irène has something of the Verdurin about her. There'll even be an orchestra, Russian music. A quartet or a septet—a sonata? To relive Proust would be very strange, with S as Albertine . . .

11:10 p.m. There was none of this, only the boredom of an almost exclusively female gathering. He was not invited. I'm discouraged. He knows I've been home since last night. No calls, not even while I was out tonight.

Tuesday 31

Just as I was about to compile all the signs that proved he'd decided to break up with me, he called. He's coming at five (I'm a little afraid he'll be reluctant to come inside if the painters are still here, which is possible). Intense desire keeps me from working. I can barely even mark student essays.

9:00 p.m. He just left. I feel even more dejected than usual, if that were possible. His laugh is almost childlike when I ask if he has another mistress. The scene in the armchair is the most beautiful, always, and I know he loves for me to caress him, slowly, from head to sex to knees, as he lies half naked, and to kiss him. I also know it's because he's a Soviet that I love him. It's the absolute mystery—exoticism, some might say. But why not? I am fascinated by the "Russian soul," or the "Soviet soul," or by the whole USSR, at once so physically close—culturally too (in the past)—and yet so different (I don't have the same feeling about China or India, whose "otherness" is more radical—a racist sentiment?). But when, *kagda* (will our next meeting be)? There's no reason he has to take his wife to Brussels, but I think he will, he's so afraid of my clinging to him. It's obvious.

Before he arrives, I'm rushed in my movements, indifferent to anything that might happen to material things (I might break a precious object, for instance), and to obligations (writing letters, etc.) because nothing but desire means anything to me now. Before, on coming back down to earth, I felt deflated, sad, and astonished at the blind haste which had taken me nowhere, because desire once appeased proved to be a vacuum. Now I accept, and even take pleasure in both kinds of time. I see the time of desire, rectilinear, and also the time after desire has gone (I'm alone, tidying things up), aimless and diffuse (the best proof of this is that I am writing about it here). Knowing is a great strength and also a form of pleasure.

February
Wednesday 1st

He serves himself whiskey (which seems to have decisively replaced vodka as his drink of preference) while I work in the kitchen. My mother used to do the same. Slave mentality—I've got it in me too. Why does he like to, need to drink when he's with me? Not that I mind—he's bolder, he lets the mask fall. How had I forgotten that moment in the armchair when he smiles to himself, showing all his teeth (which are small and slightly cruel), a sign of intense joy, as I open his dressing gown, preparing to caress him: that naked face. My pleasure makes him happy too, infinitely excites him. Dear God, it takes so long to learn the other's body and how to give it pleasure. Lesbians choose the path of least resistance.

Sunday 5

He calls, and talks at length! I'm amazed he doesn't hang up after two minutes. I tell him, in passing, that we don't have the same sense of beauty, there are differences between us. (What drives me to widen the gap?) He replies that we do have things in common, many. But what is he alluding to? Only sex, I suppose, the same violent desire to make love, or does he mean ideas on politics, too? Or, more generally, points in common between the French and the Russians?

Tomorrow he leaves for Brussels (I'd have so liked to go with him...) and won't be back until Friday. Brussels, where I was exactly three years ago, in numbing cold, and which I'd have loved to see again, with S. That woman, his wife, is exasperating. She must not like sex, so why does she latch onto him and follow him everywhere . . . ? (Like my dog-in-the-manger attitude with Philippe.) "I want you," I tell him over the phone. "Ah!" he says, embarrassed. A strange conversation, in which I make him listen to things that people are not supposed to say. "Is it better for me to tell you, or not?" "Yes," he says. "'Yes,' I should tell you, or 'yes' I shouldn't?" "Yes, tell me." But it's obviously the first time he's heard these things over the phone. Maybe he's unconsciously waiting for me to initiate an erotic exchange (this remains to be seen).

Having spoken to him is worse than silence. I realize just how much time there is to fill before I can be with him again. My life is hollowed out by desire and pain. Is that what passion is? I'm not sure about that. Because I often (no, not often—sometimes) see him the way I did at the beginning, in the USSR: a very handsome young guy, quite lacking in character, and eager to please the Party leaders.

Monday 6

It's amazing, the constant errors of chronology I make in writing about this affair, in a certain chronology of my feelings, the reality of our relations and external events. So when I recall Héloïsa Freire's show opening, it seems to me the affair was already on the decline and I was very unhappy that day. However, that was November 17, two days after the wild night when his car did not start, and a few days before the evening at Irène's. Therefore, what matters is not the *reality* of our relations, but the way in which I perceived them: I was a little unhappy then, yet I remember nothing but unhappiness. In Marseille . . . in Cognac . . . in La Rochelle . . . It was only in

Lille, on October 1, that I was truly unhappy, completely consumed by desire.

Friday 10

Dreamt about him. That makes three times. Before that, never. Meaning? A form of detachment or of acute anxiety? He is becoming something already lost and so I suffer less. From everything, his silence, for example. "I'll call you as soon as I get home." But does he know the exact meaning of "as soon as"? He must have got back yesterday. That's time enough. Dominique L talks to me about Havana: little nightclubs which are almost completely dark inside. You eat and don't know what you're eating, you embrace in the dark without seeing the other person's face. Later, all afternoon and evening, I wondered if S went to those clubs when he was in Cuba. And so his liking for darkness, which I thought was of a Freudian nature, may date back to Cuba in '75. I yearn to know. People outside of this affair teach me things in spite of themselves. (Dominique L must have thought I was fascinated by what he was saying. That is true, but not in the way he thought.) I'm torn between the desire to revisit Cuba with S (to make love in the dark, turning off all the lamps, everywhere) and that of initiating him to light, on his body and his gestures.

Writing like this fills me with waiting again, with longing for him. It fuels desire. François Mitterrand: "Youth is the time we have before us."

9:00 p.m. He called at ten past eight (the leitmotif of these pages). I no longer know whether "I believed him"—but this turn of phrase is meaningless. I'm in a world where the possible, the real turns out to be as insubstantial as the imaginary. The certainty of his visit on Tuesday cancels out my desire for hours.

Sunday 12

What I wrote above is not really accurate. Desire returns quickly, absolute, and keeps me from working (or is it that I want to preserve the desire and so I do not work?). Am afraid he won't be able to come, and that there's too much time between Friday night and Tuesday, and other things could arise. I think of his voice, that dreamy, drawn-out way of saying "yes," the Russian way, which to me is reverie and sweetness, and then, conversely, other words that are too rapid-fire ("what are you doing?"), too brief. Really, all that is irreducibly beautiful is the fact that he's a Soviet.

Monday 13

Since four thirty, a terrible anxiety that he'll call tonight or tomorrow morning and say "I can't come." So I'll go to Carlos Freire's opening, then I will have time to finish my article, and then I will be mad with despair. It's Valentine's Day tomorrow. So I envisage (for example) that he'll prefer to dine with his wife. Passion, again. Yet many flashes of clarity. But such daydreams, too—for example, when I read in a newspaper, "If, through some extraordinary circumstance, you were to have a child after forty . . ." I am on the verge of tears, as if he'd *really* called to "beg off." I think first of catastrophe (at what time of my life did I start doing this?).

Tuesday 14

Tonight, I wake up and remember the February day, a Monday, when I had a date with William R and he didn't come. My girlfriend (!) said: "He stood you up! He was sitting in a café, watching you go by!" I don't remember my thoughts that morning when I set out, full of hope, except that the street near the library was gray. I was twenty. Today, I'm forty-eight and haven't been stood up—he'd phone to notify me. I've become a person whom others "notify." And yet, there's always the same anxiety that he won't come—or, for that matter, that he will, and I'll have to face the moment when he's suddenly there before me . . . the first gestures, that elusive moment when we move from one world to another. I dream of endless desire, without the always-unavoidable, necessary conclusion of orgasm.

That he's coming today, on this Tuesday of dazzling sun and a very blue sky, is so beautiful that I won't really believe it until *after*.

Quarter to six. What if he doesn't come? Like that time in February 1961? Then, I naturally broke things off. Would I do that now? The sun has set. I haven't done a thing all day.

11:10 p.m. It's been forty minutes since he left. I've tidied up. The hopelessness of it all—of happiness and loss, I mean.

It's a stupid life, obviously. Four hours together that passed more quickly than any of the times before, maybe due to the change in our routine: a move to the room downstairs where the television is. The sofa is more intimate. He lets himself be worshiped, a little drunk, as usual. A dearth of imagination. I'm totally besotted. Watched *César and Rosalie*, seen with Philippe in Geneva in the summer of '72, and again last night, here with S, sixteen and a half years later, while making love. The film seems very old, very bound up with my past but otherwise of no interest. S really thinks in terms of "liaisons" and "mistresses." Fatigue and pain of separation that nothing can alleviate except a more sustained presence, which is impossible since I live in Cergy, not Paris. Since he did not know it was Valentine's Day, his visit has zero value as a sign. It was beautiful however. And I had no other thought in my head but that the time was drawing to a close. Terrible.

Wednesday 15

Dreams, nightmares, one in particular: I have to go into a "little box," they will give me an injection and it will all be over. This morning, disgust at my arms, which are withering. It's either that or get fat, fill in the flabbiness with flesh and be covered in cellulite. He repeated, "I am happy to be in your heart," meaning "instead of in your book," because for him that is all that matters. For the first time I'm faced with my complete lack of worth, living without writing and waiting for assignations that are nothing but a terrible descent into death. In four hours I see time slip away, as life does on a larger scale. Writing is just the opposite, the absence of time. And yet I yearn to spend a whole night with him. I don't remember why I'm learning Russian (it's crazy—too difficult), or why I'm going to write about perestroika for *Europe* magazine, or why I'm even writing about this thing, my bond with him, which does not exist.

Thursday 16

This morning the thermometer reads 37.2°. I am stunned, my mind a blank. This very clearly means that I made love yesterday, or rather the day before, in mid-ovulation, a fact also noted (again unconsciously) in the soreness of my breasts when he touched them. What is the meaning of last night's terrible fatigue? I read the description in the dictionary ("cervical permeability," the implacable advance of the spermatozoa, so intense), overwhelmed once again by dismayed fascination in the face of this blind phenomenon. Nine or ten days of terror to get through, just like twenty years ago. But did I not have it coming, to some degree? Yet I'd resolved to take the pill again, when my next period comes—if it comes now, obviously.

Sunday 19

Friday, in Paris, twinges in my belly, and the absolute certainty that I've been "caught out." Then, sensibly, I tell myself that the unconscious mind is not enough to influence the course of a Nature disinclined to act when one has passed the age of forty. Apparently, the chance of pregnancy is one in forty-five. Still, I think of S much less and wonder if, obscurely, all I expect from a man is to be fertilized like a bitch and then show him my teeth.

Monday 20

Nonetheless, as of tonight, it will be six days since he's been in touch with me. If six turns into seven, or eight at most, and not because he's traveling, we'll have moved into a new stage of indifference. Last night was difficult again. I imagine his body, always—the dimple! Discovered just the other day, the dimple on his chin. *I did not see it!* You sleep with a man and don't see that! But it's a good thing, fundamentally—it signals trust in the imagination, and what does a dimple or a scar matter? Not seeing means passion. I was thinking earlier about this trace I've tirelessly left behind me since age sixteen, my journal.

Tuesday 21

We've reached a milestone: today marks *seven* days. I spent a difficult night in a haze of despair. I want to end this unraveling affair. For instance, not go to the Soviet film on Friday (I haven't yet sent my confirmation). I'm also aware of my folly, never following through with a relationship. Am I even capable of doing so?

10:00 p.m. He calls from a public phone, which isn't working. Now I know because of the time of day that it's *him*. He can't come until next week. The words are always the same, "You're well?"—"Yes and you?"—"I'm fine," etc.

Friday 24

Last night he called but I can't have him over, Éric and David are here. Tonight was the film screening. His wife not there—"she's a little under the weather," his usual phrase, which doesn't mean anything. Unless she's pregnant . . . Watched the Russian film, sitting next to him. I only caressed his fingers. I drive home very quickly, playing cassettes with the volume turned up all the way, the song "Éthiopie," and I understand, I remember my "lust for life" at eighteen, the despair that lay beneath, the same as that which I feel tonight, at forty-eight. All because of a man. And when I see him there, in the hall of the embassy, he seems forgettable—a pretty boy, nothing more. I'm rereading *Anna Karenina*.

Didn't do anything today (the text on the USSR is harrowing). Had a misadventure with the pregnancy test, which I bought at Auchan and dared to return (the instructions were missing). Was humiliated by the girl at the information desk, who loudly asked, "Is it a pregnancy test?" and sent me to the main cashier with a credit note reading "early pregnancy test." So I didn't buy another. I'm still waiting. Tomorrow I go to Rouen, and on Sunday the big German woman arrives. Finally, on Monday, he will come. It's not much of a life, and yet . . . The Paris-Pontoise motorway, the A-15, in recent years, has been the site of infinite, unparalleled happiness and pain. Summer '84, winter '88–'89: those frozen years of marriage.

We exchange dreams and desires, he and I. But not the same ones.

Monday 27

5:35 p.m. Waiting. A memory from five years ago, my mother at the Pontoise hospital, from which she never returned to this house where I am now. Soon his car will arrive and the time that leads to death will begin. (I'm not pregnant.)

10:35 p.m. How can I say this? It's as if I were forgiven, the evening with S was so passionate. After five months, the discovery of new pleasures (though I'm always the one who leads). I think of nothing, submerged in flesh and sweetness. We lay together half-asleep in front of the television. He likes anything that highlights his manhood and his narcissism (I jerk him off from behind, he watches my hand, I'm invisible), discovering eroticism, its world of possibilities.

Tuesday 28

The day after. A night full of dreams. I cannot shake the memories, which are clear (the one described above) and hazy, both at once (I think I remained in his arms for about four hours, with brief interludes in which I went in search of things to eat, or coffee). His Russian underpants: so moving, and likewise the singlet, white, Russian, similar to the ones worn by the men in the Leningrad–Moscow train.

10:30 a.m. I can't think of anything worse than writing about the USSR. What true thing could I possibly relate except how, one night in Leningrad, I fell in love with S in a sad room where the sink didn't even have a plug.

Evening. All afternoon, I revisit those two scenes in which he leans forward to watch my hand jerk him off (I am behind him). I sense he has rediscovered a state of mind from adolescence, maybe earlier—a fantasy. I'm happy to help him to relive it, plunge back into his childhood with him. Another image: my father on his bed, two days before he died, his head bent forward. Men watch each other and we watch them? Role of the initiatrix, the mother who dispenses pleasure.

March
Thursday 2

I am really *drunk* after making love the way I do with S. The day after, and even yesterday (though differently), I was assailed by images, erotic and insistent. Only today is my mind almost clear again. But does that drunkenness—making love—leave marks on the psyche?

Last night, he called. It was very gratifying (what a word!), bliss, for me—only two days after our last meeting (gratitude? Maybe, *mozhet byt'*, he's not capable of anything more than this memory of sex—but am I?). I sense that his greatest desire is for me to publish a book while he's still here, so he can be proud of me, that is, of himself.

Sunday 5

I'm in a bad way again, anxious about the writing of this article on the USSR, probably because I dread others' judgment and may not have anything to say about perestroika that has not already been said. Besides which, he hasn't called, but that's only to be expected. I am an erotic diversion in his life, nothing more. Can I say he is anything more in mine? But what beauty there is sometimes. And how can I experience, today, something that just happened on Monday, and pursued me all of Tuesday and Wednesday, without nostalgia, without memories?

About this article: I constantly struggle against the urge to do nothing because I see *everything* that needs to be done. I cannot imagine a *timetable*, a slow succession of words and sentences that fill up time. I have no *patience*.

Monday 6

Everything is hard. Tonight I waited for his call in vain. It is 11:00 p.m., I'll read *Anna Karenina*. I've barely started the article on the USSR, and I see to what degree writing has another meaning, how much of it is transference. The first sentence is "So, I'm back in Moscow again." This is a sentence I'd like to be writing now *for real*, not ascribing it to the past, as I do in my text. This is writing as desire. It's not always that way.

Of course, a week ago, I was sure of his desire. For him, a few days have to go by for a new meeting to happen. This journal will have been a cry of passion and pain from start to finish.

Wednesday 8

An excruciating night (and evening). Sleep impossible. I'm in a hole, that is, submerged in the awareness of not being loved at all, and of having been dropped, perhaps. Awareness of the pain which this will represent, and already does. And the horror of writing an article I agreed to do for a man who no longer even calls me. My situation is as crazy as it always is when it comes to men.

He called at eight thirty. How astonishing to observe the (literal) insubstantiality of a voice and at the same time the importance it has acquired in my life, of which he has no clue. Maybe Tuesday. Me: "If you can't before . . ." Him: "It's a little difficult" (= it's impossible—I know how to translate the Soviet language).

Thursday 9

Tuesday is impossible because of Éric's Capes.* The morning is already black at eight o'clock. Naturally, I can't contact him to let him know. Soon it will be three weeks since we've seen each other, which for me will have been nothing but unremitting pain, or a sense of indifference, like that which prevailed in my relations with P for two years, from '86 on. I can see myself then, in the streets of Paris, with no desire for anything, half-dead, heavy. This is a notebook full of sorrow, with a few glimmers of wild delight.

---

* The secondary teachers' training certificate.

Friday 10

Splendid weather. I am very alone. (But my suffering, like my happiness, is linked to my condition of being a single woman. In a marriage or common-law union, it would all be boredom and jealousy, pretty much.) All the Peugeot 405s or 505s that pass make me think, "That's S, for you": a guy with a big car, social-climbing, narcissistic, for whom I only matter as a writer he's had sex with; a beautiful woman, too, who makes him hard, who makes him come, when the spirit moves him to pay her a visit. Constant, latent suffering. If he doesn't call by Monday, it may be impossible for us to see each other all next week.

Sunday 12

The elections. The last time I voted was October 20. How different things are now in my private life. I am extremely pessimistic, that is: prepared to hear (= sure to hear) a vague promise of reunion, the kind J. Brel refers to in I-don't-know-which song. I'm suffering a thousand deaths to write this article on the Soviet Union, but wouldn't it be worse to not have *anything*? The absolute freedom of the Other is dreadful—the bond with him too. Will he call tonight?

Eleven o'clock. No. Everything is infinitely difficult: correcting essays, studying a few words of Russian (to what end?). There's no point in telling myself that his intellect is unremarkable, his personality conformist, etc., since it's not these things that make me attached to him, it's that indefinable bond of flesh, the lack of which is killing me.

Dreamt of my mother last night. We were on a train. She was no longer crazy but had her face from before, from the late seventies. I don't know if the dream was consoling in relation to my life of now.

Monday 13

Will I ever finish this piece for *Europe*? It's absurd because the only true thing I can say about the USSR is that it remains mysterious and fascinating to me. Other than that, it's just the things everyone talks about, free speech, struggle, the uncertainty of perestroika. I wake up in the morning with a sense of horror, thinking that I won't see S until I-don't-know-when. It would be better if he didn't call tonight so I wouldn't have to tell him he can't come tomorrow (Éric and his Capes). I'm sick to my stomach and have the runs. Why?

In his eyes, I have no distinguishing features as a writer (he cannot really understand what my books represent, or where they stand in relation to the rest of French literature), I'm a writer like any other, in other words, I can be replaced by any woman writer of equal weight in terms of social fantasy. I'm at the end of this notebook and am about to finish *Anna Karenina*. Fear of the pain returning, worse than what I've experienced since October. I've no illusions, he'll dispose of me little by little. Or else I will have to guide him toward confession. For the duration of our affair, except for the first time, it's been me who has done everything.

10:30 a.m. He called around 6:00 p.m., when I was out.

Nothing since. My joy has steadily unraveled and left me with the following certainty: he called to say it's not possible tomorrow. I can no longer live in this kind of pain. When he calls me, I'll hint at breaking up. It seems as if I've been devastated every night for the past ten days, maybe more. The other evening is so very distant and unreal.

Tuesday 14

Slept very badly, sore throat. I've no desire to work more on my text, which is finished and abysmal. I'm overwhelmed by anxiety. A phone call: it's the painting contractor . . . How am I to *live* this way, to survive after what seems to me an inescapable breakup, or rather a logical ending to this story that was so beautiful, so perfect at the start.

10:30 a.m. He called. His car is being serviced. All at once, a kind of order is restored, which I know is false and illusory (he doesn't love me any more than he did before he called, and I have to type this awful piece about the USSR). But still, I might sleep . . .

Saturday 18

I finished *Anna Karenina*. The final pages, the walk toward death, are sublime, with a kind of interior monologue.
No word from him. Last night, in bed, sleepless and in tears, I too would have liked to die, but did nothing about it. A terrifying image: he was dancing with women from some

kind of delegation (like us, in the USSR). I was excluded—always the same story. (And how I suffered from that, on the evenings when Philippe didn't come home . . . so it was hell? Or anyway, not *worse* than now, just identical? I remembered the room in Bordeaux and discovering the blood on the sheets from that girl's deflowering (Annie who? I've forgotten), my pain. February '64. What a business that was, life with Philippe, solely based on inner lack, my need for a man who didn't love me. S doesn't love me either, never has. And what I love in him is his youth, and the USSR, which has always fascinated me, and which, right now, seems to me the subject the whole world is wondering about. It's only been four days since he called—forever. I think back to Tuesday and see myself again at the florist's in Cergy-Village, having flowers sent to the actress in the stage version of *A Woman's Story*, and I tell myself that at that moment, when he had not yet called, I was unaware of how happy I'd be that evening. But it's as if that phone call had never *happened*, was just a trifling incident in a prolonged period of pain. Having nothing to do intellectually is *worse*.

Sunday 19

He called at five thirty. Something falls afterwards, like a curtain on the piece of theater I've been playing in my imagination for days. The (calm) waiting begins, the fear, too, of seeing his indifference, boredom, the *less desire*—the last time was so beautiful. Yet the absurdity of this liaison, its "contingency," is so obvious. What binds us to each other? For me, it's emptiness, I know. And for him?

Tuesday 21

Spring, yesterday. These three weeks of not seeing him, have, without my awareness, brought clarity of vision, or indifference, as far as I am concerned. His face seemed to me banal. I found the stands he took—in favor of the death penalty and the laws against homosexuality in the USSR—difficult to endure. And yet there's still a desire to bind him to me, through the ordering, this morning, of the book he wants for his birthday. His slender body, not very manly, is so moving. Will we have our one night together before we cease to desire one another? He promised to invite me to the embassy film screening. It meant a lot to me, as the saying goes . . .

Friday 24

Dream last night in which I say: "Sex has always been a source of anxiety in my life." Since Monday, I've felt disenchanted, devoid of passion, and certain that he's not at all attached to me. As a result, I can no longer keep this thing going—not alone and at arm's length. I still think of him all the time, but without the former violence, the craving.

Was at the Russian church today, on rue Daru. It was a shock to see the architecture of those churches again, narrow and closed, and the icons. After that, I went to the exhibition of costumes, Russian of course, at the Musée Jacquemart-André.

Sunday 26

A fog through which all one can see is the magnolia in bloom. Easter. Six months ago exactly, at around 2:00 a.m., I was swept unawares into a love story with a Soviet whom I thought I was only "having it off with" for one night. Vulgarity has never saved me from anything, nor has cynicism. I'm more romantic than the most wildly romantic schoolgirl. What do I do now? Accept things the way they are and mortify my flesh (by getting laid less and less often), or break things off in my usual way? Without being sure he wants to see me again, considering his pragmatic, unromantic attitude. Him: "If she doesn't want it anymore, too bad." He's certainly very conceited in this respect, as well as socially (always keeping Alain Delon's visiting card on him!). Why do I always become attached to the vainest of men!

Monday 27

A grueling dream, the most grueling kind of all, about the death of a child, David. Then another, which I take to be reality, that is I consider the previous dream to have been a dream. A fire. The alarm is raised on time, I find myself in a room, trying on underwear. I pass the window and see the survivors (there are no victims, in any case) in a bus. They see me in my state of undress. I reflect then that in the bus, these people look like Russian dolls in a shop window. In both dreams, my parents are alive. This chain of generations is always very present in my mind (and has been since my abortion in '64).

Fear of April. A notebook filled in just five months—that's a first. A record I've never broken, not even in '63. This only proves I'm more analytical now and more used to writing. But it proves nothing about the force of the obsession itself.

Tuesday 28

9:00 p.m. The weather is just like summer. I don't think I've ever seen it this hot in March (no, I have, in 1961). It's been eight days since he called, and now one day more, and I view it all with a kind of pain that is very familiar, but from which there is no way out, since I'm still unable to bring myself to break up with him. But maybe he's decided to do just that, in his own way—break up, little by little. What if he's not at the film at the embassy on Thursday, or if he ignores me? I'm not doing another thing. The article on "politics" holds no interest for me. This morning, in front of Notre-Dame de Pontoise, I step on the exposed and twisted root of a tree, and in so doing make a little jump. In my mind, I see the summer palace of the Tsar, near Leningrad, where there are buried water jets that soak you if you happen to walk over them. I've never given them a thought since the last time I was there. One day, I'll return to Leningrad, as I've returned to Venice so many times, but by then I'll be an old woman, and I don't know how to say *tempo fa* in Russian.*

The thing which, at the time I started this notebook, I thought must happen, the gradual fading of desire, has indeed come to pass, through an inexorable process. What now? I'm still unable to extricate myself from this passion. Does this

---

* *Tempo fa*: long ago.

mean I require even more obvious, clear-cut signs that I'm clinging to him for dear life? Do I go for broke and write him a farewell letter? At times, I seem to bump up against the same listless obstacle, the same indifference in S as with Philippe. "You're leaving me? Oh."

This letter would be the end point. Which is why I lack the nerve to write it.

Nine forty. He called, we're seeing each other Friday. Am I crazy? No.

Thursday 30

It's already summer. I'm going to the Soviet embassy and I'll see him. What I love is the tension, the desire, and pleasing him. To be loved, loved, and I know that's impossible.

Evening. One disappointment after another. As "diplomat on call" he can't attend the film. He promises to join me anyway, but doesn't see me in the dark and leaves. He's not coming by tomorrow, but probably will on Monday. That caution and indifference in front of everyone! Tonight, I really did not *see* him, could not imagine in him the man I make love with. However, since I've got back home, I want him all the more, on account of his cold, reserved, official facade. Now he readily acknowledges Sakharov—and soon Solzhenitsyn too?

What will happen to me in this notebook? I would like *to hold on to* S as well as write—is that possible? My dream: a holiday with S in Moscow, a more "evocative" place than here.

April
Monday 3

Twenty-five years ago, I'd just arrived in Sainte-Maxime. Éric was conceived in the Hôtel de la Poste (?). I can picture the room and remember some of the exchanges with Philippe (me: "We are auto-erotic," he: "Ah well, some do it in bed, we do it in the car!"). And so my life was spoken for. I didn't want to be an unwed mother (as people said then) nor have another abortion. Marriage was the only solution.

Today, I don't know if S will come, if I fully grasped the arrangement. It's probably the last time before my trip. The weather is gray and cold. Will it be less silent than the other times? But why imagine that he can change? He didn't say anything in Leningrad, or in Paris, at the studio, in October. He was, is, pragmatic, and uncommunicative in the extreme. Maybe just in it for the sex.

5:00 p.m. What if I'm mistaken, and the meeting is not a sure thing? Since a minute ago, I've been convinced that I ought to have understood something different, that he'd call on Saturday or Sunday if he were coming (and not call if he wasn't). I'm in a hole.

10:45 p.m. He really did mean today. He arrived at five forty-five, after the phone call from Marie-Claude V. Her brother Jean-Yves has a brain tumor. I can picture him in '63 at Marie-Claude's wedding, our conversations that bordered on intimate. Though I often feel as if my life were ending, the actual death of a guy of forty-seven seems to me unfair, unthinkable. But I thought only of S. Who still had not arrived. I saw the blue car turn into the drive. The other time began, and ended. Scarcely a word was spoken, as usual. I ask, "Do you like this [what I was doing right then]?" He has a smile, a look, impossible to describe—of exultation. The only progress made is the light that we keep on, and the open eyes. He was happy with the book I gave him, flipping through it with the joy of a child. Perhaps I should not have added other books, as if to deny the merit of his own choice (the book he wanted). In the two other books, I dread having left a personal mark of some kind, as I sometimes do. Maria, or Macha, the wife, the *zhena*, always suspects (she has memories of me, and I'm suspicious too). Fellatio, anal sex. He thinks of himself first (that endless narcissism), but I like to give pleasure, now. I won't see him for the whole next month.

Tuesday 4

I'm in a psychologically comatose state. It's April and it's snowing. Last night, I dreamt of S for the first time after spending the evening with him. In the dream, the computer room was set up for him as a studio apartment. Abundantly clear, as usual.

Me: "We really enjoy ourselves together, but what am I to you? Nothing?"—"No no."—"No, what?"—"You're a lot." That was my reward: *a lot*. Nothing more.

The awful, silent moment when he gets dressed in the bedroom. One by one, sedately, each piece of clothing goes back on, the same ones I'd made him drop four hours earlier. First the underpants, then the undershirt, the trousers, belt, shirt, tie, and shoes (he never removes his socks). This ceremony shatters me. It's the final departure in infinite slow motion.

A dog barks. I'm at the very heart of emptiness, as in Sées, in London, 1960, or at P's in '84. I cry a little.

Something of a gigolo: he drinks half a bottle of my Chivas, asks me for the pack of Marlboros just opened. I'm both mother and whore. I've always liked to play all the roles.

I'm jealous of women who speak Russian, as if they had something in common with him that I never will, even if they can have no other bond with him. It is this *lack* in me that makes me suffer in relation to others (similar to the sensation I had at the Globe bookstore, and more recently at the Russian Orthodox church, hearing people speak this language I don't know).

Saturday 8

I have been ill with a raging throat infection since Wednesday. Disenchantment returns (the illness numbed me) with the prospect of this long journey to Denmark and the Eastern Bloc. I don't think I'll see him before I leave. Maybe a quick call, Monday or Tuesday night . . . Fog.

Wednesday 12

Malmö. I'm in a state of immeasurable fatigue. Disgust with life overwhelms me in a Swedish design shop, Silversberg. The idiocy of talking about literature for an audience strikes me all at once. Why am I here? To "take advantage" of these trips. But I pay for them dearly.

I doze off for twenty minutes. Last night, the ritual call from S: "An-nie, how are you?"—"I was sick." (Don't ask me what I had.)—"You're not going away?"—"Yes."—"When? . . . When will you be back? . . . I'll call you Saturday. Have a nice trip." I feel as if I'm seeing these words from a distance on the screen of a computer or a Minitel. And yet I never stop thinking about him and telling him everything I do, as I'm doing it. (Four years ago, it was P whom I was thinking of when I was here. Who will it be four years from now?)

Thursday 13

In this room at the Neptune Hotel in Copenhagen (the same hotel as in '85), there's the New Testament in the bedside table drawer and cassettes of porn films on top of the TV set. I wonder *when* I will dare to play one (because it will be written on my hotel bill, in full evidence!) so I can finally see what it's like. It's not to compensate for lack, but to learn new things. Maybe tonight or tomorrow morning, after the conference is over. The silence of this bright little room is absolute. Denmark, squeaky-clean and dispiriting, is like cotton wool inside of which I can no longer feel anything at all.

Yesterday, for the first time, I wanted to insult the people who came to hear me speak at the Cultural Center, I wanted to say, "What are you waiting for? What have you come for, a cultural Mass? Bloody imbeciles, there's nothing to see, and it's not you I write for, you old highbrow Swedish grannies!"

Saturday 15

Yesterday, visited Horsens and Jelling, the graves of the first kings of Denmark. Describing for the sake of describing—pointless.

Françoise A's exasperating attitude toward her boss, a woman with the "simplicity" of the bourgeoisie; hence, the constant droning way in which FA calls her by her first name, "Annie" (I may not have been as sensitive to this were it not my name too).

But the important thing is that S did not call as promised. All my hopes (frankly insane, given the state of our relations) of seeing him tomorrow are crushed. Perhaps he actually did it on purpose, precisely so I wouldn't ask for anything tomorrow. It is quite horrible now to really see the indifference he must have harbored since about December.

Monday 17

Cergy station. Later, Prague. "In . . . , I was in Prague," Camus [Apollinaire]* . . . (The sense of going to a country that is closer to S than Denmark, and it will be my first time there.)

Last night, he phoned, a neutral call to fix an appointment for the morning of my return. It is always he who decides, monolithic. I constantly revisit that first time in Leningrad, the *gesture* which set it all in motion, as the thrust of a knife unleashes horror. In this case it led to happiness, certainly,

---

* Guillaume Apollinaire, "En mars 1902, je fus à Prague." The opening of the short story "Le Passant de Prague" from the collection *L'Hérésiarque et compagnie.*

but also unhappiness. I also picture the erotic scenes that lie ahead. When I stop doing so, it will mean I don't need him anymore.

Wednesday 19

A false start on Monday, I missed the plane. Yesterday, a detour via frozen Vienna. Prague superb and black. The castle and the cathedral seen from the Charles Bridge look like something out of a tale from Hoffmann. The hotel is noisy: the Centrum, near the tramlines, with a little lounge, like in Moscow at the hotel for the central committee of the CPSU. Last night, as I fell asleep, frozen beneath the quilts that kept slipping off, in the brown-yellow room with windows that did not properly close, I felt certain I could *never* live in an Eastern bloc country. Yet people are happy there. Here, with the cultural advisers, I talk a great deal about the USSR, the Russians' pride at being the biggest, strongest country, along with the United States, and their contempt for those they crush. Also, conversely, their acceptance when they "get walloped." In some elusive way, I *understand* the nature of S's relations with me: verbally simplistic, conquering and brutal—they cannot be otherwise. I hope the cultural adviser will not divulge what he has probably guessed, that I am having an affair with a Soviet. Secrecy is always better.

The airport. I have lost my voice, am voiceless in a way I haven't been since '69. Twenty years! This morning, interview with the stuttering red-haired translator. Visited the Writers Union with "Brat," who was the official "purifier" after the Prague Spring. The atmosphere was very Eastern Bloc, the dark room, the coffee served, the impenetrable ideological divisions. Brat speaks out against Hrabal.

At the University of Prague, there were the usual attacks against the Nouveau Roman, and the mention of communist or assimilated writers. How could it be any other way?

Evening, Budapest. Earlier: a state of dereliction. I sat on the toilet, sick to my stomach, bent over a towel spread on the floor, trying to vomit. It was probably the goulash broth that wouldn't go down, too fatty. And I'm particularly fragile right now. What if I have AIDS? I could only have contracted it from S.

Saturday 22

Budapest is over. I drag myself through these conferences out of brute necessity. The cities are my reward, the dreamed-of cities that are there, very naturally: Budapest (the castle district, the panoramic view from the Liberty Statue), Warsaw (reduced to a historic site). Hatred of the Russians is everywhere, especially in Poland, in its sad and backward state (work horses, the girls looking after geese, churches), its shortages of everything (petrol and cheese this morning). The wife of the cultural adviser gets on my nerves with her jeans-and-sweater look, no makeup, but so finicky about the bourgeois education her kid is receiving, classical records by the yard, etc.

Dereliction (within limits) has ceased to make me panic. At Warsaw airport, weighed down with packages, I fall and lose both shoes. But then at least three men help me to understand the PA announcements in Polish. The plane is delayed (for two and a half hours) and in the end, the luggage does not arrive, the conveyer belt is blocked. Finally, I go to eat canned ham with people I couldn't care less about, that cultural-adviser couple. I am sick and tired of travel.

I'm at the oldest hotel in Krakow, where Balzac went to meet Mme Hańska. Thirty-three foot ceilings, false luxury, the smell of paint. Hotel Pod Różą, "hotel under the rose."

The later it gets this evening, the further I slip into a state of diffuse pain. The image of S and me in Leningrad is over-powering, the waiting to see him impossible to bear, and I weep—from loneliness too.

Monday 24

My time here is almost done. I'll give no more lectures. This kind of self-display is horrible. On Sunday afternoon, I was irritated in the extreme by the behavior of the cultural advisers E and VC toward their daughter, whom they are rearing according to bourgeois principles to the point of caricature. There is something atrocious about that cajoling violence that never lets up. Don't pick up the olives with your fingers, wait for our guest to start eating, etc. She is four years old! And their hateful blackmail involving the Smurfs: "One day I'll have a beautiful car and I won't let you get in it," the girl said, play-fully; "If you don't let me in your car, you won't be going to the Smurf film this afternoon." All said with terrifying calm. Class hatred? No. A struggle between vulgarity (me) and distinction (her, the cultural adviser's wife), which makes for irreducible divisions. How horrified she was to see me chatted up, that evening, by two Poles, who were indeed quite vulgar.

Visited, with them, the abandoned Jewish quarter of Kazimierz. There were names on some of the doors. Today, visited churches incessantly full of people, for Monday Mass . . . Poles are in the churches and the shops. They go into *all* of them, looking for whatever might be interesting. A strange ant-like busyness, the search for things to bring home with them—indefatigable. The queues are slow and mute. Docility, silence. And the church.

That way of gazing at the windows: tiny mounds of sweets, bottles of fruit juice in orderly displays. A kilo of tomatoes costs the same as a doll, and four times as much as a shampoo and blow-dry.

Tuesday 25

Warsaw–Paris flight.

Yesterday I dozed at the hotel in the afternoon. People's footsteps in the pedestrian street: strange, like a single step pounding the street over and over, going nowhere, like the shuffling of horses in a stable at night. A silent step: the Poles do not speak, anywhere. Silent queues, a stream of speechless tourists on Marieki Square. Docile and mute. There was a nun at my lecture! The church was oppressive. At the hairdresser's: nice girls in dirty smocks, a row of battered helmet hairdryers, a pockmarked mirror that presents only a blurred image when the hairdresser asks me to check my eyebrows, which she'd just plucked. The blow dryer does not heat up. Dim lighting—it's almost dark. People stop in front of shop windows no bigger than the windows of a dwelling, where packs of juice and sweets are displayed—luxury in other words. Nowhere else has the desolation struck me quite so much as here.

Friday 28

He came yesterday, around eleven. Desire. He kneels to kiss my sex, which he hadn't done since Christmas. Lovemaking was quite tender, and he still desires me just as much, but I miss words more and more. The words and tears that I repress, my eternally smooth and smiling face, my constant tenderness become unbearable to me over time. I brought him a carton of Marlboros from the duty-free shop. He instantly pulls out a pack (so he didn't bring his own? He's used to being served at my house) and will not forget the carton when he leaves. I gave him two letters (hand-written), one of which I wrote when I had the throat infection, the other in Budapest. But what does he think of them? I'll never know that either. In the evening, there's a film on at the embassy, *Assa*. I make a greater effort to understand the Russian than to follow the story line. His wife is sitting next to me. I don't "sense" anything, other than a sort of curiosity, but the few words they exchange relegate me to my condition of foreigner—twice over. She no longer seems to suspect anything. How does he make love to her? She is short and flat-chested with a big behind and hips. Does she have orgasms? Perhaps because of this vague jealousy, I had a harrowing dream: he tells me that he has spaced out our meetings several times over so I'll grow detached from him, and this time is the last. Besides, he's leaving France. From behind the barrier where I stand, I try to see him pass, but the road remains empty—I won't see him again. Is this an expression of my desire, *the imaginary solution* that would be best for me?

No sooner have I returned from my trip, freed from the obligations of self-representation and work, than I fall back into obsession and the desire to see him.

May
Monday 1st

I rewatched our home movies from '72–73 and '75. For the first time, I see myself as *other*, very different from what I am now, undeniably younger, and severe-looking. Nothing in my face speaks of happiness, especially in '75. A "frozen woman," indeed. My books have always been the truest manifestation of my personality, without my knowing it. How oppressive that marriage was.

9:00 p.m. There was a phone call but no one on the line. Am tempted to think it was S calling from a pay phone that did not work, as is often the case. But wrong numbers do exist . . .

Wednesday 3

Thursday is in a long, long time, and he never calls. I'm going to have to break up with him, my life is just too stupid. W*ho* am I working on this suntan for? And the letter I'm writing in my mind is intended, more than anything, to make him reject the breakup. I have reread the previous notebook and, curiously, am convinced he cared for me until about March, when three weeks went by without our seeing each other.

Resolution: if he doesn't come to Cergy before I leave for Jersey, I'll see him once again, and then break up.

Friday 5

When I'm in Paris, as I was today, to meet with people—the Freires, the Swedish journalist—and I see cars go by, driven by men who have a city look, the tie, the light-colored suit, the *bcbg* haircut, I tell myself that this whole story is extremely dull and commonplace. A man and a woman meet from time to time just to sleep together. It's as if all the imaginary pageantry were falling away. I'm not sad about it, since it's me who sees, who feels things this way, on my own, and not, for example, through adopting his point of view. Then I come back here, to Cergy, and I cannot bear this waiting for him to call. It's been eight days, as of tonight, we've moved to the next level. I'm alive without living. When will I break through the paper hoop, be ready to go through the pain?

Saturday 6

A dream which wakes me up. I'm waiting (for whom?) in a sort of covered courtyard. People are coming out of a theater, after a performance of *A Woman's Story* with Micheline Uzan. I see my mother there among the spectators. We talk and she says, "Was that my story you told?" I protest, "Not really." It is my mother from before the dementia, with a gray suit and a "coiffe," as she used to say, referring to her hats.

I lie in the sun, inanely tanning, as in '63, in Italy, when I was waiting for a letter from Philippe. Did I wait a fortnight, or more? The memories are fading. S is all that matters. All the power of the attachment that binds me to him may lie in his secretiveness, his unpredictability, his "foreignness."

Review of the possible causes of his silence:
1) a scene with his wife about past film screenings at the embassy, when I was there and she was not: about whether he'd concealed from her the fact that I was attending
2) his jealousy of Alain N, to whom I offered a lift home in my car
3) he's tired of me (see: my dream), and he has chosen to dispose of me by spacing out the meetings
4) work, unknown occupations (is he with the KGB?)

He *didn't say he would call.* (In spite of myself, I think of my mother, the last time I saw her, in April '86. I said: "See you Sunday," and she did not reply.) However, he did ask me if I was going to the Salon du livre, meaning that we wouldn't see each other before then.

And yet, and yet, what tenderness, the last time. But, that's just it: the last planned meetings have the beauty of things that are ending.

What if I were *never* to see him again, as with Claude G in the past? That is like death. I fear the worst (he's leaving France, ditching me, etc.).

Sunday 7

Nothing. An ocular migraine from lying in the sun. Then I'm as if crazy, depressed in the extreme, and scared. The time of day when he still might call is past. I think about tomorrow, why wait? I'm sinking into something that is uniformly painful. I had no control over anything with S, and now he'll even be the one to initiate the breakup. Passively, of course.

Monday 8

The more time passes, the more I think it's over, and that the deep reasons for the breakup will always remain unknown to me. My disgust with every sort of occupation (gardening, etc.). Constant anxiety. I'm at the point where I regret the happiness of October–November, for which I pay too dearly now. I almost look forward to my trip to Jersey as a kind of deliverance—I won't be here waiting for the phone to ring. Another possible cause for the breakup: E's gossip, slanderous rumors about me.

Evening. He called, sounding very "normal." My imaginary constructions collapse. I feel sleepy. I don't want to break up, not until the next time . . . But how am I to believe that people can love me, become attached to me? It's as if only my parents could possibly have done so.

Wednesday 10

I'm leaving for Jersey. Again I dreamt of S and that we were making love. I also had insomnia. His wanting to see me doesn't mean he's not tired of our relations. Maybe he only *maintains* them because I'm a "writer."

Friday 12

3:30 p.m. S hasn't called yet. I'm in exactly the same state I was at age twenty or twenty-two after a sleepless night. In Jersey, I didn't sleep a single minute in that icy room that looks out on the sea. It was impossible to escape from thoughts of the night before, with HS, in the Chinese restaurant and then the taxi. I'm still as powerless as ever in the face of desire. I kissed him, left his hand on my thigh in the cab. But I refused to let him come up to the guesthouse. As usual, I know that it's not *him*, HS, whom I've got under my skin, but the *other one*, S, the Russian (as it was P and not GM in '85). I've already forgotten his gestures, and all I want to do is sleep, in tears, because S does not call.

11:45 p.m. He came and stayed five hours. It had been a long time since I'd experienced such perfection, and since we'd been so attuned to each other. Made love, four times, in different ways. (Bedroom, anal sex after many long and slow caresses—downstairs sofa, missionary very tender too—bedroom, so moving: "I'm going to put my sperm on your belly"—the sofa, doggy style, so perfectly in tune.) An infinite need for the other's body, his presence.

I wake up at six. For the first time, I weep without pain over his definitive departure in August. I truly *realize* that one day he'll no longer be here, that I'll probably—certainly—never see him again. The full strength of the passion that has occupied me since the end of September appears to me now: all that beauty, that perfection (I am crying as I write this). I feel that the next book will be *something for him*, even if I don't write about him. For the first time, yesterday, we found a perfect common rhythm. I'd never found it with anyone before.

Yesterday, we argued over the reconstruction of the time in Leningrad, our schedule for the two days there. He wanted to read my journal. Again we talked about Stalin and the war. His father was "decorated" by Stalin . . .

I don't want to do anything or see anyone. There's no need now to change the furniture, imagine buying winter clothes. Something ends in August. All that I'll have left is writing.

But we still have a few months, about two and a half. *Laissez-le-moi, encore un peu, mon amoureux**—Piaf's song.

This morning, while driving through the streets, I could not stop crying, as when my mother died, or after I had the abortion, walking in the streets of Rouen. It is the main arc, the unifying thread of my life's secret meaning. The same *loss*, not yet fully elucidated, which only writing can truly elucidate.

---

* Leave him with me a little longer, my lover.

Tuesday 16

I ~~live for the sake of living~~ right now. So I won't lose anything of pure life, of this passion that will disappear this summer. How will I get through it? In about the same way as I did at twenty, twenty-two.

It's hot this afternoon. I'm eating chocolate. Immersed in heat and chocolate, I find my old exam papers (for the *baccalauréat*, the qualifying year for university and my BA). I know at once that this sensation was the very essence of my ennui, the disgust I felt toward life then, unaware that thirty years later, the same sensation would, on the contrary, be the very essence of my pleasure in living (or in having lived, or to still be living).

It's now that I love love, and making love. It's not a sad and lonely thing anymore.

Even so, even so, how to deny that he does show signs of attachment, of jealousy too (re: my suntan, the fact that I gave Alain N a lift home . . .)? But in a few days, it will all be different again. I will wonder if it wasn't *the last time*.

Thursday 18

I did not go to the opening night of the Salon du livre, where he is right now. More or less voluntarily, I excluded myself from this lewd drunken party of everyone-who's-anyone in Paris, for fear of doing something untoward, at the risk of leaving him free to meet someone he fancies. I relive all those parties I did not attend—the school of agriculture ball in '57. As on that occasion (though this time, I do not lack *the dress*, that all-important dress for dancing in), I'm home alone in a dressing gown, but a "deluxe" model (the dressing gown from '57 was pink wool, a sort of coat, with buttons), imagining the party where I will not be. Oh Pavese . . . The sounds of the party do not reach me, however. And I know what disappointment I might have felt in being there. I used to imagine something out of a dream, absolute happiness. Today, I've excluded myself because I've known too many failed and painful parties.

Still, all day I asked myself whether or not I would go. I have to *get through* this evening without suffering too much. Try telling myself that he might, or definitely will, look for me. But also tell myself, as a counterbalance, that he'll be tempted by press attachés and certain women writers who grow passionate at this gala evening, as everybody knows. Last week, did I not let myself be kissed by HS, and was I not quite attracted to him? It's poetic justice, then. Which is of no consolation at all.

Friday 19

The pain came in the night, waking me up. It has not left and will not leave until he calls again, that is, in a period of time which is impossible to determine. My jealousy, this time, is without nuance: everything's behind us now, and he knows I can no longer surprise him. The basis of my jealousy is knowing that I have nothing left. Again the temptation to break up, to try to make him suffer, if that is possible.

Saturday 20

Because Claudine D tells me that people shun the Salon du livre and "no one" goes anymore, I feel more serene about last Thursday evening, as if there were a link between people's general behavior, an atmosphere, and things which solely depend on individual will, a question of chance in two people meeting: S and another woman. I've never been able to make a separation between a man's feelings for me and his social milieu, which surely must influence his feelings. I've never believed that romantic sentiment is a force in and of itself. It's greatly affected by social environments in general.

The pain of seeing cars drive by, or even just to hear them. It all conspires to evoke freedom and pleasure from which I am excluded, and a vague suspicion I have of S, that he is making a date with another woman. But when I know he's really coming, that he's on the A15, my mind grows empty, except for the thought: he's on his way, end of story.

Sunday 21

The Salon du livre. I didn't go. Empty evenings. What if he wasn't even at the film at the embassy on Thursday—or if he has someone else? In the end, there is something adventurous about this painful waiting, something *full*.

I wake up at six and know my pain, like Julien Sorel. I go back to sleep, dream of a flirtation with a very young man and am awakened by a cry (in my dream no doubt) of "*Maman!*" It's me being summoned in this way. All of this has to do with HS, in Jersey. I have such a strong impression that for him, I am *the mother*.

Yesterday, in the metro, I was in a state of painful nervous tension, as when I traveled to the studio on the same line to see S. But then it wasn't pain I felt, just desire like an arrow sure of hitting its mark. This time it was excruciating lack, a void.

Why doesn't he call? Always the same question and never a valid answer. What if I don't even see him at the embassy on Thursday, and he's left for Alsace with his Dutch girl? Or if he makes no attempt at all to fix a meeting?

Evening, 10:00 p.m. Nothing. Or rather, there was a call and I got to the phone too late. Probably wasn't him. Or was. What difference does it make?

Memory of Tours, 1952. The luxurious restaurant dining room. Our tour group on the one hand, the country bumpkins; and on the other hand normal customers like the girl with the suntan and her handsome father. She was eating what I later learned was yogurt. Bespectacled and pale, with my disheveled perm, sitting with my father and other people from our tour group that got off the bus, I discovered the reality of difference, the two separate worlds.

Tuesday 23

10:40 a.m. No more waiting. It's been one day longer than last time, an infinite descent. Ten minutes ago, I muttered aloud, with horror, "I've got to end this." I'll go to Reims, come back, and maybe (at worst) won't see him at the film on Thursday evening. Little by little, I'm overcome by the atrocious thought that he has returned to the USSR, suddenly or without wanting to tell me, which would explain the passion of our last meeting.

Thursday 25

6:00 p.m. I'm living in a stupor. My strongest premonition: he won't be at the embassy tonight (because he's left France, or is traveling—or because he doesn't want to come, but why wouldn't he?). Another possibility: he'll show indifference and not fix a meeting with me. Or: he will want to see me. But these thirteen days with no word from him leave me little hope of that. Yet right now I don't know anything. In two and a half hours, it may all be over. My last letter will remain in my handbag. It always feels like a kind of death.

Eleven. There was a bit of everything: jealousy, the feeling of exclusion, and, for a few seconds, the end of the affair. A young woman, tall, blonde, flat chested (between twenty-five and thirty—next to her, S's wife looked withered), whom he clearly wanted to seduce. She was with her husband, the head of a tiny publishing house and probably with the CP. With the two couples, I was a fifth wheel. In addition, my presence seemed strange (to S's wife and the other woman, who immediately detected a bond between S and me). I leave, alone. I can still see the embassy carpet, the stairs I descend while thinking, "Well, that's that." I'm *already* in the future, without him. Contemptuous of him, but of myself most of all. And then, at the bottom of the stairs, did I turn? Yes, probably. I saw him coming down alone. I looked at some flyers on a table, casually. He knew I was waiting for him, of course. "See you next week."—"Yes."—"I'll call you."—"You'll call me." Then: "Can I give you a letter?"—"No." I closed my bag (which I bought for 1,500 francs, to please him—when will I stop being crazy?). So that is how it went. Tonight, I'm repelled at having gone to that inept Soviet film. *Maybe he didn't want me to come.* And maybe he won't call. The *only* positive thing was the risk he took in coming down the stairs after me, when everyone had just seen me leave. Really, the only thing. So. What about me? What should my course of action be? Break up with him—threaten to break up—say nothing? Those are my choices.

Eleven thirty. He calls. Nobody on the line. It's him, of course. The phone rings again: "Are you well?"—"Yes."—"Can I come tomorrow at ten?"—"Yes." And there I go again, played for a fool.

Friday 26

He came for a short time, two and a half hours. But that's usual, in the middle of the day. I feel as if I've done everything I shouldn't today, driven by my old urge for destruction. Told him

I'd wanted to break up last night, told him what I once told Ph and P about that Sunday in '52, then about '58, and the abortion. Enough to give him a scare. And indeed he left right after.

I'm very tired. This morning, I half-waken inside a sun-filled dream in which I feel that the organization of the world escapes me. I feel the entire painful mystery of life and the world. Then the image of S appears. He is going to come today, but that is no great promise of happiness.

Me: "Tell me if you want to break up, just say it, because I don't understand anything." "Yes, I will tell you." These words chill me. Perhaps he will say them in the coming weeks.

(About the publisher, I had it wrong from start to finish. He's not from the CP, he's the son of a bourgeois and he's going to marry the woman who was with him. S, therefore, could not have wanted to seduce her. His eager attitude can be explained by that stooge-like, Dostoevskian side of his personality.)

Saturday 27

Intellectual work is the only thing in which I can really lose myself. I'm really feeling very low. Everything casts me into despair: the vision of this past year of illusion, starting early last October, the state of subjugation in which I've lived, and now, to top it all off, the prospect of breaking up. I must, in fact, not only get used to it but want it, for the sake of my equilibrium, which now appears to me nothing more than a state of indifference, a dead state, which I therefore do not want. Yesterday, I chose the middle solution: threatening to break up. I don't know what the consequences will be. Either pride (his) will prevail and precede my manifest desire to separate; or he won't want to surrender the pleasure and the sense of pride that I provide. Judging from his behavior with people (eager to please in the extreme, almost a stooge), maybe I should be harsher, even cruel: would it pay?

Another source of pain: I cannot give up *writing the world* and for two years, I've done nothing. I can no longer live like this. Men and writing—a vicious circle.

There are *two* things I must do, go back to rue Cardinet, the site of the abortion, and go see the nurse who cared for my mother: that conjunction again. At least lift the shadow that's been lying over me for eight months, that gentle green-eyed Soviet with whom I have learned to make love less like a barbarian. In the words of Proust, "*Intelligence* opens a way out." ("Wherever *life builds walls, intelligence* opens a way out.") Perhaps get to the point where, like Swann, I'll say that I wasted my time and money (almost true) for a man who, unlike Odette for Swann, was my type, but who was not deserving.

Tuesday 30

May has been awful. When does this feeling of helplessness date back to—'85, '82? I think it was worse then. Everything to do with my marriage stirs up a feeling of horror and pain with no way out.

Moments of clarity: It's obvious that S is tired of me. Conversely: on May 12, his passion for me was clear.

Marie-Claude called me. Jean-Yves died last Friday. I sometimes think that we're mysteriously linked to other beings and that their death produces "waves." Friday, the day when I was so feeling so low, when I seemed to be lacking in every way, was the day J.-Yves died. I never saw him after July '63. He told me: "I have no friends."

June
Thursday 1st

Saw *Too Beautiful for You*. Nothing about it resembles my story and everything does. As I leave the cinema, I know it's about me, and ordinary life and the contradictory relations between men and women. And I'd have liked not to have to leave the cinema and for this story not to end. Art as a shortcut. Phrases from the film that I could have said myself: "It's nice to wait for a man," and about noontime meetings in motels, "There are people who don't need to eat lunch." And then, "I am a woman who lives. I am a woman who keeps on living"[-Josiane Balasko, weeping].

Nothing, of course.

Saturday 3

I live in a state of anesthetized pain. That is, I no longer expect anything *better*. And as hope is impossible, the pain cannot be an impulse toward a still-conceivable happiness.

I know where he is this weekend. In the Loiret, near Châtillon-sur-Loire, whose main street I can still picture, sloping upward toward the church, and the charcuterie where I went with the children (when was the last time, in '84, '85?). I know who he is with, the E family. So I imagine, imagine, over and over again.

Things whose odor brings to mind that of sperm, once hated, now intoxicating. May 12, "Can I put my sperm on your belly?" Forever ago. These memories are torment each time I think: he won't be coming to see me anymore, will no longer say those words in a blunt, Russian way. I measure the strength of my attachment through my taste for or loathing of sperm. Hence, a violent loathing with P, starting in '87. And in Leningrad, the first time with S, the desire to spit it out in the sink.

The consummate happiness: a call from S during the night from the Loiret. A little like, *Ah! If only the sun could shine tonight* [P. Tilman].

Monday 5

Dreamt of a kind of hotel, or the Châtaigneraie clinic, and I've forgotten my room number—62, or 42, or 63? People are waiting for me, hence the panic. I wake up. Every night now I'm awake between 3:00 and 4:30 a.m.: a difficult time. To put myself back to sleep, in my mind I went over the whole kitchen in the apartment on avenue de Loverchy. Why, I don't know. This inventory put me in an increasingly jittery state . . . I stopped at the huge china cabinet, with its heavy sliding doors.

Neither Annie M nor Frédérique L have mentioned my "Russian love" on the phone, and for me this silence is a sign that they know the affair is over (although objectively I don't see how they could know).

If I give up *understanding* (i.e., what he feels, or what a word or gesture means), I also give up passion. *Waiting,* too.

I picture my return from Jersey. I'm waiting for Éric at Roissy (there's a plane arriving from Moscow). I stay in the car in the Ikea parking lot while Éric goes in to buy something. And *I did not know* what happiness awaited me that evening, maybe the last, with S.

Tuesday 6

Dark awakenings. When did I dream that he removed his socks to make love? The meaning of this dream is clear: I am sure he has another woman (one who would tolerate his keeping his socks on!!). I waver between two hypotheses: 1) he no longer has any desire to continue our relationship— 2) He will call me as if nothing were amiss when he has the time or the desire to see me.

At a quarter past four, he calls: "Can I come over right away?" So it was the second hypothesis. I did not know this morning at the bookseller's or the thrift shop, nor this afternoon in my listless state, what happiness (?) awaited me, no more than I did on the day of my return from Jersey (even less so). Not really happiness, but surprise, appeasement. That intoxication with one another's body (at the end we could no longer climax), indefatigable. But why does he not give me time to really want him, await his arrival for a few hours, even a few days?

Wednesday 7

The usual immense fatigue. I can't do anything whatsoever. Scraps of phrases linger in my memory. It's the day-after, the hangover, not from drinking but from love. Numbness. I'm not at all sure if this is what attachment is. Am quite sure E knows everything.

Suddenly, I think of the wedding he's attending on Saturday, the people he could meet, *the dance* . . . Even when he's with his wife, I'm not sure about him. Now jealousy surfaces much more quickly, perhaps to save me from the slow disillusionment of the days when I wait for him to call. I am secreting my own antidote to love, perhaps to prolong this love through suffering.

Saturday 10

I do nothing, almost as a matter of course. The big book is still in a state of limbo. I prowl in circles around it. My optimism about S is based on nothing but a lessening of anxiety in my mental life. He may not call in the coming week, in spite of his promises. I work in the garden, I weed the slope and I remember gardening last October—in pain because he hadn't called—in the very same way. This memory of pain is sweet now because I know I was wrong, then (later he would show his violent attachment), and, at a deeper level, because

I'm having the same experience, but without the same pain. It is similar to writing.

Sunday 11

Insomnia. Once again, I conjure up the memory of Leningrad, revisit the joy and sensation of then. But for me he was still insignificant, in the most basic sense of the word: a man I wanted for one night only. All the value I attach to the night in Leningrad comes from other evenings and afternoons, the dozens of times we've made love since, and better than on that night. I'm half numb right now, with no desire to work or read, not even worried that I haven't heard from him, which has become a matter of course.

Thursday 15

The truths of first wakening, when I'm only half conscious: I'm nothing for S except a well-known woman who is a good fuck, so worth visiting from time to time. No attachment on his part. Bursts of pride, no doubt dampened by the specter of my forty-eight years.

I've completely forgotten the young man from Jersey, who, moreover, has not replied to my letter.

The brutishness of S, when I think of it—or Russian shyness. When we meet, there are no verbal preliminaries, not even hello, only bodies from the start. In October, he didn't say anything all the way to Cergy, smoked in silence, drove quickly. All this to say that I was *prey*, every time: *done for.*

Friday 16

Nighttime, difficult awakenings. First, because of this cystitis, which is torture (again . . . I've had it since October . . .). Yesterday, an excruciating trip home on the RER, because of the urge to urinate. The holding back brought on last night's pain. And S does not call. I try to work, to write, but am hounded by a devastating image: Sunday, the return from the wedding at Barbizon, S fucking his wife. I know she's not his first choice (nor am I, any longer)—she is simply there, close at hand, in the marriage bed. At least for me, he has to travel forty kilometers and build an alibi. But still. It's as if I fall into a hole when this kind of vision takes hold of me. My only comfort is to read the preceding pages, about pain that is equal, or worse. My request that he call me more often fell on deaf ears. The suffering begins after about a week of silence.

Saturday 17

Eyes closed, I think of nothing while the beautician plucks my eyebrows. At one point, I feel breath on my face and lips, regular, unsettling. It is the beautician, who bends very close to me to pluck the hairs (unlike the other women who have performed the same treatment on me). I reflect that a body is breath—life and desire have no gender. I knew it at fifteen when I asked Colette if we could kiss on the mouth "to see what it's like." It was a failure, our knowledge of each other made it impossible. I open my eyes again. The beautician is a woman, like me. It was only the breath that made me think of love, not the face. And a woman cannot give pleasure greater than that of masturbation, not like what I shared with S, on that Friday, May 12, when I returned from Jersey. The scent, the sweetness of sperm, that smell of bleach, or privet blossom, is secretly restorative, enough to make you swoon.

Monday 19

I count the days, attaching an increasingly negative interpretation to each that goes by without a phone call. But he probably has another sense of time, which he does not even calculate. Still, this lack of calculation has a meaning, that is: how little he must need me in his life.

The weather is still sunny, the sky imperturbably clear, summer has arrived early. This morning, I desperately wanted to see him, as I did CG in '58—see him and make love, even if he doesn't give a damn about me, and too bad for the disillusionment that follows, the unhappiness.

I did not at all think, in Leningrad, that S's relative youth would seem desirable. Then, it was only clumsy and unsatisfying, for one short night. This "asset" has become increasingly important, but surely less than the "asset" of his being Russian.

When will I see things with more distance? But then I'll become incapable of writing what I'm writing here, of being attentive to these shifts of feeling inside people—near impalpable, unguessed at until now—provoked by passion, desire and jealousy.

Afternoon. A terrible state of waiting, in the sense of need and emptiness. Desire that is not physical, or detectable in my body (it doesn't make me wet, for example). I'm psychologically hollow, alienated from myself to the point of weeping.

Evening. Another phase, never has so much time gone by without his calling. Did he go to Alsace? Maybe, maybe not. The horror of not knowing. I write to be loved, but I don't want the love of *readers*. I could write in a book, straight up: "Love me," like J. Hallyday in I-can't-remember-what song. And "people" would love me, certainly, the fragile woman from *Apostrophes*, or the lectures in Prague and other places. But I only want love that is chosen, desired by me, preferably for a man who doesn't see me as a writer.

Tuesday 20

Will June be worse than May? It looks that way. It's obvious that a man who doesn't call even once in two weeks has no feeling for me. Pitilessly, I view the reality of the situation and the suicidal aspect of my attitude: I do nothing to free myself from my obsession, my desire. Jealous imaginings course through my mind. Tomorrow I'll go to see the Russian film, *Little Vera*. Already I picture him accompanied by another woman, whom he kisses in the theater. He never keeps his word about phone calls. In short, I am tearing myself to pieces over a character who is quite conceited and self-assured, all things considered, whose pleasures are controlled, compartmentalized—though they weren't in the beginning. What we have here is nothing more than the erosion of desire over time. Why not gather the strength to admit it and reap the benefits, as in the past: *Je ne suis pas de celles qui meurent de chagrin / Je n'ai pas la vertu des femmes de marin* [Barbara].*

Wednesday 21

A dream which says a great deal about my desires and what I'm afraid of being: I meet S in public, for lunch. He puts his hand on my shoulder and we look for a place to be alone, and he really wants me, as usual. A kind of cave, the light inside dims, the water on the ground swells. I'm afraid, and we leave the cave. We meet back at my place, the house is full of people and the children are gone. We go to my room, the bed is filled with objects, as if I were moving house. I start to stroke his sex. A change in attitude: he becomes ironic, mocking (which he never is), reproaching me for rushing for his cock and always wanting to make him come (which is true). Later in the dream, the cat Lucrèce reappears, alive. (She has been missing since Friday, and I think she's dead—another sorrow of this month of June.)

Thursday 22

He called last night at around ten to eleven. Was he a little embarrassed (his voice)? He suggests that we meet . . . next week. "I'll call you Monday." Will he? I'm still adrift, unable to think clearly. During the night (insomnia), I tell myself that he may have been expecting me to refuse, relieved that I'm initiating a

---

* I'm not one of those women who die of grief / I don't have the virtue of sailors' wives.

breakup he dared not initiate himself: hence, my fear that he won't call Monday, but later. Then, as I began to daydream about his body, and that future meeting (further aroused, in the afternoon, by the film *Little Vera*, whose hero is called S), I was assailed by images of the dancers in Paris, those sensual, liberated women from an island he still recalls with nostalgia. In an abyss of jealousy and intense sorrow, I imagine meetings in hotel rooms, as straightforward as ours in Leningrad. Proust's phrase, which I wrote down at sixteen, returns: "Sorrows are obscure [. . .] servants whom we battle against, under whose dominion we fall more and more completely, and who, by way of subterranean paths, lead us to truth and death. Happy are those who have known the former before the latter, etc." In horror and sadness, I make love to myself three or four times. However, the sadness remains, exhaustion not prevailing over uncertainty, impossible to dispel, as to whether S is an ordinary pickup artist, or a guy to be picked up. But the dilemma is no longer relevant, for it seems that Cuban woman are very sexually assertive.

Resolutions (to reread Monday morning): if he postpones our meeting again, without fixing a date, I will suggest—calmly, without a scene—that we no longer see each other. It's a tactic, obviously, but make-or-break. If he comes but shows little desire, I'll take similar steps, directly or in a letter prepared ahead of time, which I will present to him, or not, depending on his attitude.

Monday 26

I was quite sure, from the morning on, that he wouldn't

call—I think this has happened before (early January? and in March?). The usual reason: he is unable to come around, so there's no point in calling. Living in anxiety is the worst possible way to live (are you sure of that?). In any case, this can't go on for months on end, the limit being his departure for the USSR at the holidays.

Tuesday 27

I am reliving the darkest and most inadmissible days of my life. I am *allowed* to be sad about the loss of my mother, or even of Lucrèce, the little cat who disappeared last week—but not to show that the total absence of S destroys me. Tonight, tears, the desire for death, the horror of feeling my flaccid thighs and knowing that I'm doomed to get old and therefore condemned to solitude. I will not see Gorbachev, and S has someone else: these are the probable facts. I haven't seen him for exactly three weeks, though I haven't been traveling as I was in April. The time has come to break up, simply in order to stop suffering.

Evening. Watched *Summer of '42*. All movies are about love. I'm crying now. "I would never see her again," said the narrator in voice-over, at the end. Always the same story. Mine too, maybe.

Wednesday 28

It is one year ago today that I met S at Irène S's, at around 5:30 p.m. (he was late), but did not give him a second thought. Not until two months later.

I always think I've reached the final limit of pain and then it turns out not to be true. Twice during the night I wake up and weep with such anguish that I think my heart is going to explode. It is Italy in '63 all over again, perhaps worse: the not knowing. But what is there to know? His indifference is all there is, whatever the cause, be it work or another woman. And my pride took a blow because he didn't invite me to the embassy for the Gorbachev reception.

Thursday 29

He is coming. Dreamt last night of a naked child. I am walking in Yvetot, rue de la République, going to the doctor, or is it a church? In my dream, I have a date with S, as in reality. I see a large cross, the Golgotha. Difficult to interpret.

I live in two different times, one is painful, with no meetings planned, the other (like today) devoid of thought, a stupor of desire that will be satisfied, though never as fully as I've imagined. But last night, I wept with happiness to know that he has not completely abandoned me (this sentence is appalling, straight out of a lonely hearts column).

11:00 a.m. It's raining. The fear of a missed meeting, an accident. Celebrating for nothing. Or rather, the pointless preparations: making myself "beautiful" and waiting, all for nothing, the most terrible thing of all. And every day, my mother had to wait for me like this, in the last months of her life.

Eleven ten. I'm more and more worried. The incessant noise of a jackhammer blocks the sound of his car arriving. There's always this fear before the *ceremony*, and I can't think of a more beautiful ceremony.

Noon. He probably won't come now. This June has been the darkest in a long time. I've never been so unhappy as in these hottest, most magnificent days of the year.

4:00 p.m. He came, delayed because of needing to drive someone to the airport. He leaves about two hours later. "Are your sons jealous of me?" He too wants to be the preferred one, arouse jealousy . . . But he's so much stronger than me. Almost exclusively concerned about his career. Unless he's hiding his true game, that is, seducing women. But isn't his fear of people finding out about us the sign of something unusual in him? And those socks, higher today, just below the knee, dark-colored (making me think of my mother's . . .). The question remains, what binds him to me? It isn't just pleasure, which, in a manner of speaking, is part of the past now (therein lies the drama). Quite simply, he is who he is, and he's been in my life for almost a year, but not enough, that is just the problem. Why do I systematically avoid recording, here, all the signs that could serve as proof of his attachment, when these are the things I tirelessly reminisce about? Is it so as not to record *all* my weakness in this journal? For example, my desire to interpret the question "Are you going away on holiday alone?" as a sign of his jealousy.

Friday 30

Wrote ten lines on Gorbachev for *L'Humanité Dimanche*. At another time, I probably would not have agreed to do so. But in this case, it was like being with S in spirit. Similarly, this morning, for the first time, I lay curled in the sheets, recalling his body, his face, in the same bed yesterday, images of great sweetness. He has a natural kindness (perhaps indifference?). I saw him, *sensed* him in a different way from other times, feeling a detached tenderness (a trap, for me, see: Philippe, in the past).

I like it that he arrives without cigarettes—on purpose?—and asks me if he can take the package with him. Me: "Take the other one too." "Yes?" He pockets both with no qualms. A gigolo down to the last detail.

July
Sunday 2

Had a dream that woke me up this morning. It takes place in the cellar in Yvetot. A girl is trying to have sex with me, and I refuse (is it David's girlfriend—or her mother, whom we talked about yesterday?). Later, alone, in the same place, I masturbate. It was that cellar and that precise location, opposite the door to the adjoining room, to which my father dragged my mother to kill her in June of '52. Now three men, no women, know this. I loved all three men. This admission was the sign that I loved them.

I am experiencing a period of calm, as if in June and part of May, I slid to the depths of despair and, as a result, I'm able, I'm allowed to live again. Or rather, to distance myself from this life which I have lived through in darkness and at the peak of emotion—real life, but excruciating . . . Must break through the paper hoop. I also know I will relapse in a few days or weeks, when S leaves for Moscow. But the pain has begun to stagnate, it seems.

I think of '63, the ashen early days of July, after breaking away from the hectic life I'd had for the two preceding months, and before the devastation I would experience in Italy. This time, the devastation is behind me—September '88, in Leningrad. Always compare inner states, not concrete situations.

Wednesday 5

Probably because I didn't see him at Gorbachev's lecture at the Sorbonne, my return to Cergy was black. As I entered the Trois-Fontaines shopping center, just in front of McDonald's, I had a sense of infinite despair, felt the flatness of everything. I no longer *want* to suffer from absence, from desire, from waiting, and I try to think of nothing.

In spite of this limp, defeatist attitude ("love does not exist," "everything is imaginary"), sadness closes in on me at times, like this evening. I feel I am weighing the pros and cons of my previous passion. Once again, the strength it gave me seems beneficial. Does that mean I'm about to slide back into my waiting, my love (what other word is there for it?)? But restrained, this time, more disenchanted in advance? I'd like to forget the face, the pleasure, the body of S, and for him to turn back into the man who entered Irène's house last year, whom I didn't think about once over the summer.

Friday 7

Overcome by emptiness, the lack of a will to live. In the morning when I wake up, I know that I'm *in mourning* for a passion. Two dreams last night, Georges M appeared in one, but nothing else remains. The other had to do with a meeting of people vaguely affiliated with the Franco-Russian milieu. There was Irène S (seen Wednesday at Gorbachev's conference and last night on TV), S and his wife. A memory of shaking hands with them. Then everyone is walking. A young blonde woman, very tall and thin, joined the group. I think I'm jealous of her, especially when she goes to bed, naked, in some sort of sleeping bag or box. But we can see she has the genitals of a man. Androgynous, therefore. I have nothing to fear from her. Hard to interpret, unless this young woman is a double of S, who is tall, slim, and blond with smooth skin like a woman's.

I find everything difficult, painful. I'm *at the end of my tether*, unable to say to S, next time: "No, don't come." And yet I expect nothing from our meeting (it's probably the last time before he leaves for Moscow).

Saturday 8

I don't know what I'm going to start writing, or even if I'll write at all. Anyway, once again, I'll have *paid dearly* for what I write. During the night, the desire for death was so strong, the moral suffering so intense, that I understood resorting to tranquilizers, dope—anything. Fortunately, all I had on hand was a pathetic Spasfon-Lyoc. The reason is not really S (I've become a little more clear-sighted about our relationship) but the *absolute need to write*, barely distinguishable from the pain of living I've felt since the end of April. In other words, I'm in that hollow place where death, writing, and sex merge, and I see the link between them but am unable to surmount it. Spin it out in *a book*.

And there's the same old summer silence. It used to be the silence of waiting (for something to happen—to meet someone, obviously). Now, I know that waiting never leads to anything but disaster (CG–Philippe, S) and there is nothing I can count on but words to fill the void.

Sunday 9

This pain—which I am tolerating a little better today— is caused by the conjunction of two things: the necessity of writing, and lucidity about the fact that S doesn't love me. The two are linked. The *truth* had to come to light before I could write. But there is no more truth than before, only a change of beliefs. I'm just giving up passion in order to write. But the transition from one to the other is excruciating, and very ambiguous too: I'm still waiting for a call from S before he leaves for Moscow.

Wednesday 12

Noon. Tomorrow, it will be two weeks since I last saw S, he hasn't been in touch with me since. Maybe that's the way I should live: take his calls and visits as they come, without waiting, fuck lightheartedly, *e bastà*! But I don't know how to live that way, I never will, even if it proves increasingly neces- sary (does a woman have to be satisfied with that, after fifty?). I have nothing but time until September, and I won't start to write, probably because *starting* means being lost to the world for months.

Dreamt of my mother, alive and not insane. She was carrying a folded mattress, which she unfolded. Then a dream about a train, in which I'm traveling next to a guy who's deranged. I change seats.

Thursday 13

Dreadful nights, especially the wakings. Not wanting to wake up, but to plunge back into sleep until the pain has been erased and the requisite time (therefore a part of my life) has passed. And that contradictory desire to stop getting older, and the dream of sex, unquenchable desire (yes, that too, of course), most of all with S. All I'm waiting for now—the most minimal, modest and humiliating desire imaginable—is to see him one last time, if only for an hour, but with the following proviso: I don't want to see him again in September, if he returns. Because in the end I must have the upper hand, if only just a little.

On waking, I thought: "a bed of suffering." I am worthless—what am I doing, what am I bringing to the world right now? My increasing awareness of having an insane attachment to an arriviste, who is not particularly sensitive, and who is overfull of pride, especially. But I knew that *before*. These things don't mean anything.

Celebrations for the bicentennial of the Revolution have begun. I'm not invited anywhere, just at a time when I'd have loved to lose myself in vain distractions. If he doesn't call tomorrow, another "record" will be set.

I enclose a four-leaf clover in a letter I will give him (if we meet again). A lovelorn schoolgirl's mythic recipe for impossible bliss!

Friday 14

The worst of all possible horrors: celebration, celebration everywhere. The radio, television, and newspapers rattle on about the pomp and splendor, and my pain, this morning at around five, was unbearable. I did not get back to sleep. All I could see was my passion and his indifference. Pride and self-loathing unto death reduced me to violent weeping. The absolute necessity of breaking up—impossible to remember later, all memory having then turned into suffering—and all the emptiness I must assume, the negation of the past months (and desire takes so long to die . . .), obliterating my will to live, or rather to keep on living. Moreover, I saw that my intuition must have been right: "something" happened in the middle of May (like something happened near the end of November) to alienate S from me definitively.

The questions "what will put an end to my suffering?" and "what can I do to make him attached to me again?" do not have the same answer, except in the event of my having a chance to tell him that it's over. In that declaration, there is always a desire to conquer anew.

3:00 p.m. He called this morning at a moment when my thoughts could not have been darker: "I congratulate you on this anniversary!" Nice. He's coming around in a few minutes, or an hour. Life, absurd life, those things that are happening yet again. The fourteenth of July! The French Revolution versus the Russian Revolution, last November (when he came to me after the reception at the Soviet embassy). Five years ago, it was P, on the same day. It's as if men were excited by the taking of the Bastille. Ha! And I will play along. But afterwards: loss, pain, emptiness.

Saturday 15

He arrived at 3:20–30 p.m., and left around 8:15 p.m. Five hours. I feel a little less desire for him than I did last winter (November) but I always marvel at our caresses when we first meet again. Yesterday he had time, which means there were more words. Insane, dramatic fatigue. Last night in bed I was like a stone, incapable of movement. I am so thoroughly saturated with him that I'm unable to want anything, least of all writing. It had been two weeks since we'd seen each other—the average now. Eight days would suit me better, knowing that his wife (or another woman?) is fulfilling his needs . . . What did he mean by "Women are hard to get"—that he is trying without success to "get," or that he has had another woman but it wasn't easy? Or that in general he finds it difficult to seduce a woman? Before our affair, I believed that he was shy—on the Leningrad train with a woman whose sleeping car he was initially assigned to share, and with a hippie girl who asked him for a cigarette on rue de l'Arbat. But the shy ones also succeed, he is proof . . . All that said, it was I who took the lead on that night in Leningrad. This morning, I'm the way I was in '63, after Saint-Hilaire-du-Touvet, woolly-headed, feeling the shape of his body inside my body. It's obvious that nothing is more desirable and dangerous than losing the sense of self, as with alcohol or drugs, at least in my case.

Of course, the causes of my attachment are multiple, but I picture that combination in him of coarse and sweet, his youthfulness which allows me to dote on him and gives me back my twenty-year-old self, who lived in shame (whereas now I live in joy), and his Soviet nationality.

Sunday 16

To write for him. But that doesn't work any better, at least not today. I've grown used to wasting my time without fear or guilt. Tonight I was troubled by the following coincidence: on TV, a program on the Russian Church, in which a nun said that she'd had her revelation in Zagorsk, "it was as if I'd fallen in love." I fell in love too, in Zagorsk, in the Museum of Icons, but not with God.

Thursday 20

It takes hold of me again as I wake up, the disgust with life, all the stronger, curiously, for my having had no time to really think for several days (was in Avignon for Tuesday and Wednesday—a feverish, pleasant feeling in the air). Signs of desire and admiration from a boy of twenty who was handing out brochures, and the promotion efforts of Micheline V only made me desperate because my head and body are full of S and nothing else.

Rereading the notebook from last year. Things were no brighter, and very empty. This does not console me. I start to suffer from S's absence a week or six days after our last meeting. At this point, I stop wanting to write for him, I want to write to forget him, detach myself from the one who in my mind always wears the face of Vronski.

A Man's Place is very distant now. The only moment of emotion: when it strikes me that people have come to listen to my father's story, the summary and meaning of what he lived in obscurity—and painfully, I believe. (Because he was depressive, as I am, as they all were on his mother's side, the Lebourg line.) Yes, I got a kind of vengeance, I avenged *my people . . .*

Friday 21

One week. Dreamt of holidays with Danielle Lafon (who wrote to me yesterday). I have sex with a guy (a gigolo, or maybe not—did I pay him?). Afterwards, I'm dreadfully afraid of having AIDS. Then S is in the dream, but what he's doing there is a blur.

Sunday 23

Reread my appointment diary from '63, when I was waiting for Ph in Rome. Saint-Hilaire-du-Touvet was not like Leningrad, not really. But I have the same expectations, the same desire as then. Fleetingly, the self of yesterday, of Rome, is the same as today's. The two men form only one shadow, that of

S taller and softer. My account of meeting S and the night in Leningrad could have been written by the girl of twenty-three I was in Rome. I am just as lyrical and amazed as in '63. The similarity frightens me—what will become of me with S? I can't say that *men are my perdition*, it's my own desire that gets me lost—my submission to (or quest for) something terrible which I don't understand, born in the union with another body and no sooner gone.

Tuesday 25

He calls at around ten twenty, when I no longer expect a call. Such a curious impression of banality, when I felt such desire for him the night before. I dreamt of him: "What do you want to do?" "I want us to have fun together," he said in the dream, and that meant making love. I'm distant on the phone, as if it made no difference to me whether he came around or not . . . And yet all I do is think of him.

Thursday 27

10:30 a.m. A chilling thought, yesterday, "what if today was the last time?" and all night long, the question, "what is the present?" Then, as now, I was completely focused on the hours—perhaps the last—that we will spend together. And during those hours, I will feel terrible loss at every instant, except while making love.

I also know why I'm so strongly bound to S, the kind of man who doesn't really dominate me, at once distant and gentle, a

father (like mine was) and a blond Prince Charming. In Zagorsk I should have thought twice. He's so wonderfully Russian,
too, and for that reason, perfectly attuned to the peasant I still
am, deep inside.

9:25 p.m. I knew it already, but as long as things are not *spoken*
(or written down—in literature, direct and without innuendo),
they do not exist. And after that, they never cease to be. It was
a very beautiful evening as far as desire goes: lovemaking with
the TV playing (as in '58 with Dalida's song "Je pars" in the
background). He said my name and replied, "Me too," when I
said, "I love making love with you." Of course, the appetite for
knowledge, that is, for destruction, had to rear its head like an
old demon. I said, "Ya tebya lioubliou" (I love you). He answers
me in Russian. I don't understand and make him repeat it. "Only
Masha?" "Yes." Then I answer: "That is why I will leave you. But
you'll feel no sorrow because you're strong." He again answers,
"Yes." It was the moment when he was leaving. Those words,
which no others came to cover up (except "I'll call you next week,
will you be here?"), destroy me. Sobriety returns in a burst of
images: I see him as a playboy (or a Gorby boy!), a brute (though
not much of one), and a philanderer (why not). I tell myself I've
wasted a year of my life, and money, on a man who asks as he is
leaving if he can take the open pack of Marlboros. At twenty or
at forty-eight, this is what it all comes down to. But what do you
do without a man, without a *life*?

Today, I'd put on my mother's wedding ring. Afterwards
it crossed my mind that she may never have experienced the
things my hand has done (the ring is on my right hand, to
avoid any allusion to marriage, in relation to S) while making
love. Now I reflect upon the strangeness of the gesture (totally

unconscious, the product of deep, instinctual desire), which I simply saw as an action that would bring me *luck*, in no way a desecration. It's something quite apart from desecration, the ring of my dead mother being part of a ceremony of love, a kind she condemned but never ceased to think about.

He always takes a particular interest in women's ages, probably a way of expressing his tribulations about mine, twelve, almost thirteen years more than his. Even though it didn't matter in the beginning.

Friday 28

Everything's increasingly difficult to bear. However, I tell myself that it was a beautiful affair, and later I'll tell myself how lucky I was to make love so well with a handsome Russian guy. Why doesn't it make me happy? Moreover, there was emotion . . . Dreamt of a room, S is there, along with other people. The mail clerk has a package for me, which *nobody* wants to collect, it's up to *me alone* to go. It's a very beautiful green and black pen. Nothing ambiguous about the meaning: writing is everything . . . Agonizing. Probably, too, that writing is a way of making people love me, which for me means ceasing to love.

The end of yesterday's meeting cast a shadow over the happiness of what came before. For example, he takes me by the hair, with both hands, as if it were in braids, and pulls on it gently during fellatio. We look at each other a lot. In the bedroom, he seemed not to flee the mirror anymore but to seek it.

Sunday 30

Gloomy Sunday. Rain. My mind a vacuum. I recoil from thinking of future meetings, of S in general, and therefore from the analysis of what I feel. But I can't fully engage in other kinds of thoughts, either—hence the emptiness and dissatisfaction.

Dreamt I was trying to board a train with a suitcase. This takes place in the USA. The gap between the platform and step is too wide. I manage to get on the next train, with extra effort and attention, and keep hold of the suitcase. Can I keep the suitcase—S—and write?

August
Wednesday 2

A call at about ten forty-five this evening, when I'm watching *Océaniques*, Russian films from 1924 to 1928. He is coming around on August 4—an extraordinary repeat of 1963. In my unconscious mind, there's something very similar about the two arrivals, twenty-six years apart, in the intensity of expectation and desire. The relative youth of S is also significant, the permanence of the male in his sweet and virile triumph—so sweet, his skin and hair, his way of kissing me, the way I was kissed at age eighteen in Yvetot, on the little path near the cemetery, by D, who desired me as the boys from Sées did, better than some of the students in the past, and surely better than Ph in Italy.

Do I live differently because I write? Yes, I think so, even in the depths of pain. But not always: that's the whole drama.

Thursday 3

There'll be no repeat of '63. He came on the third, this afternoon, at four fifteen (stayed until 10:00 p.m.). I'm exhausted, physically, psychologically—the two indistinguishable. Dazed from the frenzied way in which we make love. Contrary to habit, he came a week after our last meeting. (I keep note of these things to make comparisons between the times before and after, of which I'm never sure.) For the first time, I want to keep a g-string soaked with his sperm under my pillow. He set upon my breast as never before, walked naked without shame, talked to me about my last letter. But all of that is still, always, a mystery to me. It is no proof of love, which naturally can't be proven.

Friday 4

A strange, almost mystical night, when physical love provoked unfamiliar sensations, perhaps similar to those which drugs produce. First of all, my arms and legs are terribly heavy, as if crushed by a truck or blocks of earth. I don't sleep at all. Later, in a troubled sleep, my whole body is buried, or rather flattened against the earth, the sky, whatever—the world. I'm united with something huge, as if I were myself enlarged, flat and heavy, but with happiness. There's no sense of airiness or floating. I am part of the heaviness of nature, wonderful—almost part of its movement. I truly *woke up* at half past seven, shattered by fatigue, without a clear thought in my head. Dramatic, needless to say.

Tuesday 8

The absolute vacuum of these holidays takes me back to the boredom of the summers of adolescence and even childhood, starting in '51 (1950 being the last great summer of play). The object was to use up time, stave off boredom with all sorts of inconsequential activities, including reading. Later, *summer writing* would assume the function of filling up dead time.

On waking, I first remember being in a bus (public transport, again!) and then of having become Russian. Consciousness returns with the words of Nizan, like a slap: "I tell you, men are bored!" I think of my mother's feverish activity, her desire to work nonstop, and my own need to *do*, but only useful things, useful to the world, especially: political writing, social action—hence my desire for commitment (even in love, I commit myself to death), the need for *praxis*, giving to others.

Wednesday 9

I dreamt in Russian, uttered Russian sentences, thought in Russian (what, I don't remember), and then I dreamt of Miss Ouin, my history teacher from the fifth to the third, at the Saint-Michel boarding school. I have a problem with my shoes, but I end up fixing it (a metaphor of "having my shoes back on the right feet?").

Yesterday I tore up letters once sent to P, which he returned to me. I was stunned to see that I had written those kinds of sentences at the same time I was working on *A Woman's Story*. I know these letters were purely conventional, but they contain no objective signs that would allow one to discern this.

My father-in-law is dead. He's being cremated this morning and I will not be there. I chose to stay home because of S, who came yesterday. What is there to write about, if not the pain—and now the certainty—of his departure in a few weeks? It all will end, the beautiful love story, the madness and the tenderness: it will all go blank, like time when nothing's happening. On TV, in the afternoon, there's *Dorothy*, *The Streets of San Francisco*, *The Case is Closed* (or something like that), *Le journal de la Révolution*, always the same programs. We make love, eat, inseparable, our sweat, our mouths joined, as we caress each other. Yes, what a beautiful story. Yesterday, I reached new heights of pleasure. On his side, there may be an element of performance. But it doesn't matter, desire is all that counts.

I haven't changed: last night, I felt just as I did after Saint-Hilaire-du-Touvet, the same phrase came to mind, "this fatigue which has something of him in it," which will disappear.

He left at half past ten, even later than last time. I'm afraid that *she* will realize.

A gray day. I'll always be twenty-two in my head and heart. Which is a drama, of course. Because I cannot, as in the past, "wait for his return" (I remember that song, "Le guardian de Camargue," which contained the phrase, *belles filles, attendez son retour,* "beautiful girls, wait for his return," and how I played the old 78 rpm for G de V in '56. Later, in '58, I played the Platters for CG, and in '63, I was stirred to hear *J'ai la mémoire qui flanche / J'me souviens plus très bien* and "La javanaise").* In four

---

* *J'ai la mémoire qui flanche / J'me souviens plus très bien*: My memory's not what it used to be / I don't remember very well.

years, I'll have more wrinkles, I'll be going through menopause, and he, at forty, will be in his prime.

"You have given me a lot, a lot," he says. I have a vague sense that he's referring to eroticism, the body. That's as important to me as anything else, if not more important.

Yesterday, my discovery of those formless underpants, evidently Russian, which remind me of the sixties: blue with a white waistband. Maybe he wears them to throw his wife off the trail . . . Or because he doesn't care about these intimate details (but that's not usually the case). And then there are the socks he keeps on, always. I've never intentionally said a single word to hurt him. Whenever something has slipped out, I've caught it in time and been annoyed with myself. Anyway, it's only happened once or twice, no more. I'm both mother and whore for him.

Thursday 17

He came three Thursdays in a row and will not be coming this Thursday, nor probably at all this week. I plummet back into a pain that comes from many things at once: the desire to see him, so intense—the prospect of so little time remaining—the vision of what days will be like, after the *nevermore* of his departure. In restless sleep, a hazy dream of my mother: she is crazy and trying to escape. She gives me a portfolio of "unusual" photos, that is, which don't correspond to reality—a photo of Geneviève at my house in Yvetot, for example. Dreamt of a storm in a house. Lydie, Philippe's wife, is there. Sexual dreams: I'm in Lille, which has become a den of delinquents, thugs, etc.—Chicago, in reality. With some very young girls, I run across dunes and vacant lots, lying down on the ground to escape the gangs, which in fact are invisible. We arrive at a house, beneath a portico. There is a boy undressing a doll, which is quite unremarkable. He penetrates her and immediately comes, as in a close-up in an X-rated film. I see sperm flow over her vulva. I am surprised that this "good" girl has let herself be *taken* (that's the term that comes to my mind) with no show of shame or sorrow. Who is she? The *old self*, the one that I was not and wish I had been, who only came into being later in life.

The annoyance of seeing Éric constantly watching for the phone calls I don't receive. My mother, my husband, my sons . . . And when Éric leaves in October, I know that S will have left too. My solitude here will no longer be of use to me.

The night of the day before yesterday, going to bed, I thought, if S has come around often in the past few days, it's not because he's leaving but because the "other mistress" is on holiday. Immediately the thought makes my blood run cold and throws doubt on everything. However, it fails to become a certainty, unlike other thoughts I've had.

Try to remember his expressions, his expressions: his close-lipped smile, or rather, false smile, when he shows desire for me

his way of shaking his head saying, "Ah! no!"

his face so soft, so childish, his lips already open when he's going to kiss me, late in the evening, when we're on the brink of great fatigue, the exacerbation of desire

his indignant "listen!" . . . (about criminals visited by popes to "redeem" them—he doesn't believe in it, an old Manichean worldview).

Friday 18

Silence for eight days now—difficult, after the past three weeks. Is he visiting André S? Does he have "obligations"? I'm recording my whole journal on a tape recorder. When will I catch up to the present, these lines written in the confines of passion? It's not enough to shorten the time of waiting/desire. It's worse than the daydream state related to inaction.

I watched an X-rated film on Canal+ without a decoder for the first time. I was at first surprised to see genitals at such close range (very clearly, especially in the close-up shots). It's very mechanical, not very exciting, and since I can't hear the words, less erotic than a book. I didn't watch the whole thing. However, this morning, the images haunt me, they're a perfect *how-to* manual. To watch the acts is far more performative than to picture them based on a written description. The most disturbing image remains the one where the man ejaculates on the woman's belly, "I will make peace, sperm, flow to her like a river" (the Bible).

Saturday 19

My terrible fear is that he'll call to say, "I'm leaving for Moscow," or "We won't be able to meet again," or that he'll do so later, when I'm in Florence. This possibility will probably ruin my trip.

Monday 21

An even greater fear that he has already left. Without letting me know, of course. Watched a program about the KGB last night. The immense abyss of the unknown opens beneath my feet: what a small part of his life I must have been! His activities as an informer (or not) remain shrouded in uncertainty. You couldn't dream of a situation more romanesque than that of having been the mistress of a KGB agent, but this dimension has not occurred to me in the past months, which may have been a mistake. What if my letters were archived, and for no other reason than as "indecent" material, Western rot.

Tuesday 22

Morning dreams, which have the merit of calming my anxiety about S: I let myself be wooed by Mitterrand, with a great deal of self-disgust and submission. We take the metro together, but it's impossible to board the train (too many people). Two trains pass, a third never arrives. We have to eat lunch standing at a snack bar table on the platform. Then Mitterrand is recognized. Another dream: P brings me a beautiful white dress from Hungary, in the traditional style with red embroidery.

Wednesday 23

This time, a dream which, when I wake up, almost makes me cry. It takes place downstairs. I sit in S's lap, writing him a letter in Russian, trying out the phrases I know. Sometimes I make mistakes, and correct them, like writing *t* instead of *m*. How clear it is in my dream! The contents? I tell him I love him, and that he only thinks of work, *rabota* . . . I turn around, and his face is so gentle, just as in reality. We start to make love on the armchair.

A gray awful day. Tomorrow, it will be two weeks, and there is almost no time left. Where is he? Here I am again in the same state of horror as in June, or worse, as in May. I do not exclude the possibility that he's left for the USSR without letting me know. Without letting me know, despite his promises, in order to avoid goodbyes. I'm driven mad by the idea, mad with pain. If he doesn't call by Saturday, this explanation should be considered.

Thursday 24

Again, I assumed the worst. At eleven forty yesterday, he called as I was reading *Le Monde* in the sun. "What is the present?" I ask myself all evening and all night long. That present is entirely present/future, now. Tonight it will be the present/past—horrific. Thinking of this gives the present I'm now living all of its intensity. It also prevents me from trying to figure out what these afternoons of making love mean to him. Maybe nothing more than that—making love.

I would have liked to write down the details of each meeting— imagined, planned in advance: 1) the dress I wore, 2) the things I made to eat, 3) where I was when he arrived (also planned). Mise-en-scènes that add so much beauty, raising life to the level of a *literary novel*. But you have to be able to afford this luxury.

It is ten past three. Still an hour to wait.

Evening, ten thirty. The present is here, limp and indistinct, the meeting over. He was in Rome and Florence! And Avignon, on the way back. Conclusion? Pure chance, or a desire on his part to know what I know too? There's no way of telling. He leaves in October. He wants to see me again in two or three years. He even says, "in ten, twenty, thirty years, the first person I will call is you."

Wednesday 30

The weather is gray and cold. The fine weather ended last Friday. I am buying things for winter, for a time when he'll no longer be here. The departure has begun. At the same time, because I'm leaving for Italy, as I was last year on the same dates, and the same atmosphere prevails here with the boys (Éric working, David having his friends around), and nothing has happened yet, I feel as though I'm about to leave for Moscow and the one-year cycle will begin again. The endless repetition of that idea.

Thursday 31

The weather was good in spite of everything, yesterday, but he didn't call as he did last week when I was sunning myself in the garden. A sinking feeling that he won't come this week, and there are only two days left before I leave. Must get used to the idea that I may go to Italy without seeing him. This morning, on hearing the song "Le petit bal perdu," I wept my heart out, not because of memories of that year when Bourvil sang it, the qualifying year for my BA, when I was twenty, but because of the imminent loss of S. In '58, I was absurdly waiting for CG. I hoped to grow more "beautiful," cultivated, and self-assured in another year, or two or three years (and it happened). Now I can only grow more withered and flabby. All I can hope for is to write more "beautiful" books, obtain more "glory." From where I stand today, this prospect has no sparkle.

Yesterday, David's friends were here, bridge, etc. It reminded me of a night in October when I hadn't received the call I was waiting for, and it was worse than now. Perhaps this passion would not have lasted long were it not for the constant pain and uncertainty. And there's always the fleeting image of the playboy womanizer that he might be, beneath his facade of awkwardness, and in spite of other signs. But the truth in this regard no longer matters. There's too little time left.

5:00 p.m. Rain. The worst part is the desire for a man's odor, like autumn mushrooms, damp and potent, while knowing it will be taken from me forever in a few weeks, along with all the things that opened up before me—Russia, the *imaginary memory* of his childhood and youth.

September
Friday 1st

Sun and wind, the beautiful summer of '89 is dying. And I say *beautiful summer* because I think it will remain that way in my memory, despite a total absence of activity and projects, other than that of desiring S.

My birthday, forty-nine, a hairsbreadth from entering my fifties: the scary decade. My wishes for this year are both simple and difficult. To write a book, the "total book," or something else, although I no longer wish to baulk at the necessity of this project, whose structure has yet to be determined. To live the ending of the beautiful Soviet love story, with even greater passion, but also to receive regular calls from Moscow, after he leaves, and not relive the excruciating vacuum of October–November, and that of '58.

He called today at around eleven forty. A kind of propitiatory sign in spite of obstacles and all kinds of distance: age, nationality, and worst of all, geography.

Monday 4

Tonight my forty-nine years barely matter. Nothing matters. There was that deep attachment, *that thing*. There were no real words of tenderness, and yet there was nothing but tenderness—and eroticism, obviously. But with him the two were never separate. I am absolutely exhausted. I will leave for Italy, as I did after Saint-Hilaire-du-Touvet, in '63—the law of eternal return? It's a question I don't even want to ask myself, tonight. Whatever the case, it is still a beautiful story.

Tuesday 5

I gave him the newspaper for the day of his birth. How happy these attentions make him, and infinitely tender. Have we come full circle? Things are as they were in October and November. "You are beautiful," he said. We caressed each other with our lips, as we did then. We have a profound under-standing. I like the submissive positions, where he completely dominates me—he sees me from behind but I don't see him. The same goes for fellatio. I still have so much trouble piecing together the memory of his face. I will lose it.

Tonight, I know I have to write "the story of a woman" over time and History.

"How long have there been these restrictions and difficul-ties in the USSR?"—"Since Gorbachev." Scathing. What to conclude?

He has come to like my height and slenderness, I think. His way of caressing my belly, so tender. His long kisses, after he comes in my mouth (the last time he did this was in December, I think). I don't know, as I revisit all this, *how* we are going to separate. *Ainsi que le coeur qui se déchire au début de l'absence,** those lines by Aragon—about the Russian revolution, so it happens—were already haunting me last week.

After what will soon be a year, we still find new ways of embracing one another, our desires endlessly inventive.

Thursday 7

Florence. Why did I want to come back here? I don't remember. The city does not compare with Venice nor does

---

* From "Tant pis pour moi" by Louis Aragon. "[Like] the heart that tears at the beginning of absence . . ."

it have Rome's memories, for me. Its only merit is that it takes me back to that initiatory voyage of '82, when I lost my husband after eighteen years of conjugal life, and gained the desire to be free. But now everything is different. I'm obsessed with a man who is leaving France and to whom I'm bound by memories of passion. Last night again, on the train, over and over I replayed the scenes from Monday and new ones I'm preparing.

The hotel is on the banks of the Arno, excruciatingly noisy, and if I had to recall a state of mind, it would be that of Rome in '63, that of "What am I doing here?"

This morning, revisited the Uffizi, *Spring* by Botticelli. The Church of San Lorenzo, pointless, Badia Abbey, where Dante met Beatrice, so they say. The Bargello museum: a superb building, the inner courtyard greatly satisfying to both body and mind. And everywhere that sensual, shameless, powerful sculpture that sings the praises of life. I don't understand Russian art—too spiritual. A hot chocolate at the Rivoire café, where there were chic Italian women, then a group of Japanese tourists (who still annoy me as much as ever). Via the Ponte Vecchio, I go to the church of San Spirito, which is closed. Dereliction in the Piazza Santo Spirito. A hippie type sits down next to me on the edge of the fountain and I feel the same despair as in '63—oh, leave me the hell alone—now, at forty-nine . . . But I don't look my age. I have the feeling this week will be very, very long.

Afternoon. Santa Croce, of which I remembered nothing except the Pazzi Chapel and the Christ of Cimabue. Beautiful frescoes by Giotto. People read the guidebook out loud for their families. What's the point? I verify everything I've learned. It doesn't really give me pleasure, but, how can I put it, the whole is beautiful, reassuring—is eternity, or almost—is humanity. A stylized, moving form of the tumuli (tumulans) of Santa Croce.

Friday 8

This morning, I come upon a Mass, all songs and candles, at Santissima Annunziata. I remember then that it's September 8, the Nativity of the Virgin. I used to go to Mass and take Communion on this day. A memory of '53: morning Mass, the weather was wonderfully hot. With my cousin Colette, that afternoon, we had a date with Michel Salentey, thirteen years older and yet my first passionate love, shared with Colette, without shame. Now there is S, thirteen years younger. I have the feeling that in 1953, I'd already guessed it all: passion, the Male. The male, yes, once again that's what dazzled me at the art gallery: Michelangelo's *David*, the sublime body in its very slightly oblique pose. Wonderful hands, so strong, embodying David's pure strength. Every muscle, every joint, the exact spot where the hip is outthrust, ever so slightly, all of it for me sings the praises of the male body, made divine by the brilliant sculptor. Some women say the male body is ugly. I don't understand them.

Tapestries on the theme of Creation, Eve's sin: fundamentally devoid of sin, very natural. Paintings from the Quattrocento, crucifixions gushing blood in a steady geyser flow. There's a baroque quality to these scenes. Later I visit the convent of San Marco and Fra Angelico, which I also saw in '82. A lovely cloister, where I remain until two. The Duomo, crushed and crushing on its stifling square. The interior disappointing—I'd forgotten. Sandwiches and tamarindo on the Piazza della Repubblica, at Caffè Donnini. The Church of the Trinità, dark. The Orsammichele, even darker, and bizarre.

The sky grows overcast, the weather cooler. I decide to finally visit the Badia Palace cloister and, for the third time, enter. When I reach the loggia by way of a dark little staircase, several people are there, gazing at the amazing frescoes: a meal, a cloth hanging on a wire, and a horrible dog on a kind of crate. Then I'm alone. Silence. There's a huge tree in the middle of the cloister. Will it still be there when I come back again, one day? A tremulous, wondrous moment: the happiest and fullest kind of solitude that can be. I find myself hoping that the wishes I make here will all come true. When I enter the church, I am surprised to find five or six people there. Don't they know that there's a cloister to see? Then my solitude of a moment before seems strange, an exception, extraordinary luck.

Tonight it rained. From my window I see the cobblestones gleam.

Saturday 9

The day was almost cold, with alternating sun and wind. No revelations to speak of, even a vague sadness. Weekends in Italy always drag me down. Casa Buonarroti, in the morning—of little interest. The Ambrogio market—pretty—and a church of the same name, then the antiques market—overpriced. What is one to buy? I'm no longer the frenzied shopper I once was, especially seven years ago. After a grueling walk through a square full of cars, I found Santa Maria Novella closed. I drink a cappuccino in the Piazza della Repubblica, almost shivering with cold. Piazza del Duomo and the Opera del Duomo Museum. Michelangelo's Bandini Pietà, in which the artist's death is plain to see. The beautiful "panels" (fourteenth century?) depicting the victory of the early humanist ideal. A disgusting scene of the creation of Eve, her body half-emerged from Adam's side. Later, the Medici Palace—useless. Finally, Santa Maria Novella, very sumptuous and open inside, the way I like churches to be (the Duomo is an empty jewelry box). A Masaccio *Trinity*, in which I searched for the Holy Spirit, in vain. I forgot to mention the Medici chapel this morning, the very beautiful groups by Michelangelo, on tombs: Day, with a blurred face, and Night, Dawn, and Twilight. This time, I've really discovered the power and the genius of Michelangelo.

Tonight I regret having planned to spend so many days in Florence. I have a tiny room, dreadful neighbors (a woman with a terrible voice, worse than my mother's; my mother at least was quiet when she was outside our home). I feel the same reluctance about eating alone at restaurants as I felt at university about going to the dining hall alone in the evening . . .

Sunday 10

A golden, provincial Sunday in Florence—*objectively* more pleasant than the other days. But I believe that my Italian period—except with respect to Venice—has seen its day: 1982–89, seven years. The melancholy I felt in Rome in '63, on July 14, I think, comes back to me. It will only be a week from tomorrow since I last saw S and he murmured, "You are beautiful." It feels very remote, more than the other times. So imagine how he'll feel once he's outside France. Over the two days he spends on the train between Paris and Moscow, I will slowly disappear from his mind, like those frescoes on the walls in one of the chapels of Santa Maria Novella, representing the earth and the sky.

The sadness that wells up in me when I hear cars pass on city streets . . . It's three o'clock. I came back to my room, well aware that I'd be quite unhappy, true to the past: a hotel abroad, afternoon, solitude . . .

This morning, at the church of San Spirito, there was a Mass. The place is unspoiled by tourists and the market. The church of San Felice: dark and tiny. At the Pitti Palace: the Palatine gallery and the gallery of Modern Art, quite abysmal (lifeless paintings from the nineteenth century). Finally, the Boboli gardens, the Cypress Alley, the Kaffeehaus full of Germans, who must go there on account of the name. A crass and tiresome couple sits down at my table (a woman alone, therefore . . .). Then the amphitheater, the Buontalenti grotto with the huge dwarf statue that S told me he'd photographed. To think that he was here, and at the Uffizi, the Pitti, the Duomo, only three weeks ago! The gardens were very difficult. It takes great strength to walk alone in the Boboli, where everything is an invitation to love. A memory of the Parc de Sceaux, last October, and the gardens of the summer palace, in Leningrad. Sometimes I feel sure—based on what, I don't know . . . then again, why not?—that for better or for worse, I'll see S again, that we'll never really leave each other.

Rain. Despondency. Dreams, dreams, of making love with S.

Last night, I decided to look for the reason why the smell of Liérac moisturizing body cream has repelled me since the first time I used it. A "hospital smell," I thought. On further reflection, having eliminated the idea that the smell was linked to my mother (which is what I thought at first), I've got the answer. It was the cream I spread on my stomach during pregnancy (for Éric or for David?) to prevent stretch marks. Disturbing. Which pregnancy (or was it both?) did I reject, struggle with? I always thought I was happy, then. But perhaps the memory has to do with physical deterioration, the distended belly, nothing more. Very powerful, nonetheless, considering the instant sense of repulsion that returns with each application. Emotional memory does not *lie*. (Really?) How could it lie? Now that I *know*, the smell no longer bothers me. Knowledge is always liberating.

1:30 p.m. This morning, I almost fainted at the post office. Muggy weather, long queue, a horrible sensation: "will I be able to hang on until my turn comes or collapse at the counter?" I sit in the telegram room and compose myself a little. What's going on, is it my period, supposed to arrive today, or is it hunger? I ate a lot at breakfast, but otherwise nothing since yesterday noon and I'm walking a great deal. Weakness (red blood cell count? blood pressure?). In this state, I went to the church of Ognissanti (the robe of Saint Francis is not tattered enough), the museum of Marino Marini (who's that?), and a tearoom near the Duomo. Rainy, sultry weather. The fear of dying here, in Florence, and never seeing S, who has suddenly returned to Moscow.

Yesterday, until one in the morning, I read Serge Doubrovsky's *Le livre brisé* in one go. It haunts me, despite the things for which I reproached him at first, the Lacanian plays on words, etc.

Evening. One week ago . . . This afternoon, in the streets of the Oltrarno district, I imagined us meeting again at Moscow airport, so vividly that the opposite scenario—the impossibility of such a reunion—seemed unthinkable. I entered Santa Felicità (a sign?), with tears in my eyes, completely possessed by him. I thought that passion, for me, would forever be Michèle Morgan and Gérard Philipe running toward each other in the last scene of *The Proud and the Beautiful* (that unforgettable music, 1955).

Enthralling street, silent and mysterious, near Santa Maria del Carmine (Brancacci chapel under restoration), with the house where Lippi was born. San Frediano di Castello, nothing to say. Strozzi Palace closed. Church of Dante, very much a mortuary. Veneration and then a tour of the house, three narrow stories (two rooms per floor).

I can't love Florence when the weather is like that of Rouen or Copenhagen.

Tuesday 12

Morning. Same restaurant yesterday as on Saturday: "Sola?" *Sola*, as in Rome in '63, I chose to be *sola*. Sentences (which I tore up) came back to me from my first novel, of '62: "She went down rue Beauvoisine . . . She . . . She . . ." The voice-over in my head says "she," I've been a character from a novel right from the start. I'm reading Grossman's *Life and Fate*. After the initial heft (eight hundred pages to be got through), I'm becoming captivated by that swarming mass of humanity, that insight. And I think, "What I've experienced with S is as beautiful as a Russian novel."

The inverse of '82: this Florence trip of '89 does not separate me from someone, but binds me to him deeply and against all *reason*.

Midday, Bardini Museum. Because it is not in the guide-book, I view the works with less attention. That is how it is with knowledge from the outside, like mine in relation to painting. However, there are many magnificent Virgins, a mon-umental Christ from the fifteenth century. After that, a visit to the market and the working-class neighborhoods around San Ambrogio, places where I always feel at home.

Evening now. A beautiful afternoon. I went up to the piazza San Michelangelo, the sun was radiant. San Salvatore, San Miniato, the most beautiful church in Florence, for me. Fan-tastic animals on the pulpit. Then—not so pleasant—walking up Via Galileo (too long) to Via di San Leonardo, which winds down between old houses where countesses have written on the walls that they once lived there. A young Italian in a fast car, always the same Don Juan, "married on all sides," tries to pick me up. *Non capito*.

The view from the Belvedere is as beautiful as the one from the Piazzale Michelangelo. I spot all the churches, Santa Maria Novella, etc. Walked down to the Boboli Gardens and the island, which I hadn't yet seen. The colors, tonight, were real Florentine hues, the same ones you see in the paintings. When I opened the door to my room, I thought I'd left the lights on. It was the setting sun.

Before having dinner in a "Florentine" trattoria (awful, in fact), I saw the facade of Santa Croce again, the square now empty. I thought, "my last evening in Florence." S was with me everywhere I went. It's a *dream voyage*, before the nightmare of real separation begins. One day, perhaps, I'll picture this room with its view of the Arno as a memory of happiness.

Wednesday 13

Another gray day.

At four o'clock this morning, a brutal awakening. In one fell swoop I *relive*, with the same force I sometimes feel while writing, the arrival of S at my house in the afternoon. I'm waiting, often in my office. All at once, a violent crunch of gravel, the sound of brakes, the car door slams, footsteps on the gravel and then on the concrete porch. The door quietly opens, closes, the bolt is shut. His footsteps in the corridor. He was there. For I live, relive it, in the past tense, suddenly. I relive it, as I will in memory. I cry as I write this, tormented by the fear that he's already gone.

Thursday 14

Yesterday, quite a sweet and lovely day of departure. In the morning, at the convent of Sant'Apollonia, saw *The Last Supper*—realistic, oppressive—and at the Scalzo cloister, those terrible, monochromatic frescoes (*Salome—The Feast of Herod*). I was the only person there. A little old woman opened it up for me by intercom. I read *Le Monde*, still at the Donnati, go back to Santa Croce. By chance, led randomly by the streets or the unconscious, I come upon the wonderful ice cream parlor from '82 on via delle Stinche. I eat my ice cream in Piazza Santa Croce, so beautiful now, without the awful parking lot where David and I made a game of trying to evade the hourly money collector. I enter the church one last time, to see the frescoes again. On my way out, an inscription, one among hundreds, stops me in my tracks: *Voglio vivere una favola.* I don't know what that last word means—an adventure? a passion? Objective chance has lit my path with its dazzling light again. I know this phrase is meant for me, right now. Still later, after the aggravating purchase of a handbag, I find Santi Apostoli, which I did not notice in the morning. One last good omen on this trip to Italy.

On the via dei Santi Apostoli, there is a strong odor of horse manure, regularly washed away by machines. A fat woman sits on the sidewalk. You can see her very clean and very white underpants, the outlines of a protuberant vulva. Since my mother died, I have ceased to look away from such scenes with embarrassment.

I'm writing all this and think, it's almost nine, and that he said, "I'll call you Thursday evening."

Saturday 16

What if he's gone? Since my return, only silence. Absolute horror of all activity. Waiting, a lump in my throat, no tears. What if, instead of October 15, "they" had decided on

September 15? Or maybe he already knew it would be September 15? According to Éric, there were two strange calls on Wednesday, therefore the thirteenth . . . My stomach churns with dread.

Maybe he is *only* in Spain, or visiting André S. But when will he be back? Or is he only waiting to find out what day he can come before he rings me? How satisfying that explanation would be, in spite of his cruelty toward me. It rains and rains, there's no more sun to help me forget and idle away the afternoon in the garden.

Evening. I received an invitation to the Soviet film in late September, but that doesn't prove a thing. I'm not sure it was his handwriting. At times I sink into a dreadful state and cannot hold back tears. The silence of the past two days, since I've been back, the fact that he didn't call on Thursday, is death—the abyss. As I write this, the certainty of his having left takes hold of me like madness, and my waiting in Florence to see him again becomes hideous.

Sunday 17

Soon, tomorrow, it will be a year since I took off for Moscow, and all that followed, that thing called destiny, which is nothing but a series of acts whereby we press on in the same direction. To understand the genius of Proust, you must have experienced *Albertine Gone*. I am truly reliving *The Prisoner* and *Albertine Gone* (I like *The Fugitive* less as a title). No one yet has said, "SB has gone," but I know that this is what awaits me if I call the embassy or go to Soviet cinema night on September 28. I am in a state close to the one I was in after my mother died. *I understand* those years of my life, '58–'59–'60, their unspeakable pain, but not the madness, then, the dreaming of a man—no more than I understand the strength of my attachment to S. Except as a way of getting closer to the return to nothingness, aspiring to primordial fusion with the cosmos (myths!). *Voglio vivere una favola . . .* What a mockery.

Evening. He called at three o'clock. After that, it took me an hour or two to return to a state of calm that resembles the one I was in before these last three days: to wash away the anguish, the death which invaded me when I thought he'd gone back to Moscow. Why do I always imagine the worst, I am forever the abandoned child (abandoned by whom? by my mother, during the bombardments?). It's not over yet, there are still things to be experienced. However, I have few illusions about the possibility of his calling me from Brussels, and even fewer about his asking me to join him (in Russian, "it's a bit difficult" = it's impossible). Today, all the signs that he would call turned out to be *accurate*.

I will have been dreaming for a year, soon. I'll awaken from my dream in a month. These lines by Racine, so wonderful, which I loved at sixteen, and can say once again:

> *Dans un mois, dans un an, comment souffrirons-nous*
> *Seigneur, que tant de mers me séparent de vous.*
> *Que le jour recommence et que le jour finisse*
> *Sans que jamais Titus puisse voir Bérénice.* *

---

* In a month, a year, how we must suffer too,
  When land and sea distance me from you?
  The day will dawn, and the day will cease,
  Without Titus ever seeing Berenice.
  (Translation by A. S. Kline)

Wednesday 20

Today, the *signs* that he will call do not pan out. He won't call from Brussels, he won't ask me to come. I have lived out this passion in the same way I write, with the same commitment, and every day brings me closer to the end, October 13, since I'm leaving for Bremen on that day, returning on the 15th, the day he leaves. Because of this, I cannot count the reasons for jealousy (who will he meet in Brussels, etc.), the inadequacies of this affair condemned to death.

Saturday 23

And so today I've caught up to the present day in entering my journal—twenty-six years of journals—into the computer. It's not much of a story, just a layer of egocentric suffering. Yet I know that it is through this layer of suffering that I communicate with the rest of humanity. I read, I've been reading, in the past few days, through a blur of irrepressible tears. S didn't call from Brussels. And he's probably back. I'm not even sure we'll say our goodbyes. I wonder if it will end up being S, even more than P, who propels me toward a "literature of pity," the wonderful pity of Russian books.

Sunday 24

Anguish. So little time, and no sign of life from him, life that could be restored to me for a few days or hours. Dreamt that I was going to the embassy for Soviet cinema. *A Woman's Story* was being shown in Russian and the actress was not Micheline Uzan but an actress of no consequence. The staging was atrociously realistic, and *every* part of the story was *performed*. S does not sit with me. People are pressing me to discuss theater with two or three Russian writers, including Bitov. Marie R is there. I have the impression that I'm going to be invited to Russia.

At about two or three this afternoon, it will be exactly a year since the moment when I first desired S in Zagorsk. I can picture the icons, my blue fleece Sonia Rykiel dress, the "gallery slippers" on my feet. I *feel* his arm around my waist. Suddenly the thought "why not him?" occurs to me, divides the trip into a before and after, makes a definitive cut in time. That arm was still unknown, was not the arm of now, naked and soft.

Monday 25

Three weeks ago, there was still happiness—on that Monday. In three weeks from now, I'll have nothing more to wait for: he'll have gone back to the USSR. My despair at having had no calls since the Sunday before last has grown into a frenzy of pain. My throat is seized with anguish, tears, and the horrible fear of not seeing him Thursday at the embassy, or of his ignoring me like the time in May (I was wrong, but then I couldn't tell the difference between reality and appearances—and besides, which "reality"? . . .). Michèle G's happiness, yesterday, her anticipation of an affair with KG heightened my pain. Last year, in October, it was me who was starting a love affair, whose excruciating outcome was naturally to be expected. But going to the ends of misery first means going to the ends of happiness.

Yesterday, it came to me with certainty that I *write* my love stories and *live* my books, in a perpetual round dance.

4:40 p.m. Three weeks, as of Monday. So many meetings, and then nothing. I have not been so *low* since the time of my abortion, those days of waiting for a solution, at the end of '63. The horror is in the *not knowing*. I'd prefer he call me now to say he's got someone else and that it's over between us. I've always preferred to "face my destiny head on." I'm doing nothing, absolutely nothing. Even gardening is abhorrent. The worst part is going to the embassy on Thursday without his calling me before. I don't feel like doing anything, as when my mother died, and I can't write a book about him (I promised him I wouldn't—wrongly, no doubt).

10:00 p.m. At around 2:00 a.m., a year will have passed since I pledged my life to passion, in two seconds: there was only a moment of *repentance* in front of S's door, at the Hotel Karelia. I woke in the middle of the night, last night, and thought, "The train has stopped." I thought I was on a night train, undoubtedly the Moscow–Leningrad train from that night last year. Time has stopped. Every night, for the past few days, I've felt that I don't care if I die. I never saw G de V again. And I never saw CG, *who did not come to say goodbye* in '58 as he'd promised to do. And S?

Tuesday 26

An almost sleepless night, with several dreams. In one, I'm going down rue du Clos-des-Parts, where the housing has become very dense, as in a pedestrian zone. There are a lot of people just outside my parents' grocery shop. I'm wearing a soiled skirt (the black one I wear for gardening), which explains my deep embarrassment. Another dream, of gay men signaling to each other (the return of Mishima's book, *Forbidden Colors*). I get up and put on my mother's wedding ring (in reality, not the dream!) as a talisman. I need something to hang on to. And I constantly repeat to myself: "Truth or death." I must, must know what's going on with S, and not keep on living in this extraordinary state of anxiety.

Thursday 28

10:10 a.m. Last night, there was a call at ten. So for twelve full hours, "I've had something." I mean that the waiting to see him is a possession, a piece of property, and that the rest of the time, "I don't have anything." All I can do is "be." So difficult. Right now, I'm not thinking of all the things that usually obsess me: Does he have another woman? Will this be the last time? Yesterday he seemed curt, preoccupied, or indifferent on the phone.

2:00 p.m. Sexually, things are still positive, but why kid myself? *That's all there is*. As he got dressed in the study, gazing at his back, his buttocks, I was overcome by a sense of desolation, or rather of deterioration, which leads to hatred, for having lost so much time since March, when my course on Robbe-Grillet ended, on a man who only sees me as a piece of ass and a well-known writer. As he sat at my desk, he tried to read what I've been writing, which I may insert in the thing I haven't started yet.

What lies in store for me this evening? Because despite his wish for me not to go to the embassy ("I will not be there," "the film is mediocre"—truth or lies?), I'm determined, once again, to "face my destiny head on."

11:00 p.m. Destiny is hazy, the signs are not good. He was *there* and not at the Bolshoi Ballet. The film was mediocre indeed (we did not stay until the end). Masha wasn't there . . . A meeting planned, from which both wife and mistress were to be absent? He keeps looking at a woman, tall, thin, blonde, mature . . . His type? Given that he loves the take-charge kind of woman, as if I didn't know . . . Today, a new position: interesting, both sitting, backs toward each other. Don Juans are all I've ever known.

Today, I feel certain that he often lies, with every appearance of sincerity.

Friday 29

The endings of my books, except for *A Man's Place* and *A Woman's Story*, have often been flat and pointless, the writing breaking off rather than ending. Perhaps, contrary to my desires, the *S novel* will end that way too. Yesterday, my discouragement and self-disgust as I watched those stupid game shows with him on TF1, like *The Price is Right*. I discovered just how unintellectual he is. Same thing in the evening: the Russian film deserved to be watched until the end. He was prodigiously bored, kept fidgeting, nervous in a way he almost never is.

I was unable to end things at the right time. That would

have been around Christmas, I think. It would have been difficult in March because of the devastating spring.

October
Sunday 1st

When this month ends, everything will be finished. There will be silence. No more "Annie" with a Russian accent, no more waiting for the sound of the car, or footsteps in the afternoon. I go back in time: a year, one year ago, on October 1, I was to see him again on the following day in front of the Église de Saint-Germain-des-Prés. I think he was wearing jeans and a green polo top—I'm no longer sure, but he was smiling. I already liked him quite a lot. He was going to be very much in love with me, then grow bored, maybe "cheat on me," and leave. How simple it all is, and October has come round again, with blue asters in the garden and the smell of earth. I'm in a state of latent pain—the kind masked by analgesics, if the pain is physical—and tormented by three dreadful thoughts, 1) that of never seeing him again, 2) that of having "wasted" several months on an unrequited passion, 3) the humiliation of being less desired and less admired, compared to the first months. My nighttime awakenings are black.

Thursday 5

Already I'm in the separation phase, the worst, the one brought on by lucidity: I should have broken up with him at the beginning of December. But that is absurd, since I can't help believing and feeling that July and August, especially August, were *good*. And because even now I hope for at least one final meeting. But what am I to think of our last meeting, his lies about the film, where he was not supposed to be? I'm now convinced that he's had other women at the same time as me, but starting when?

Don't think back to this time last year. Try to survive. I hate to think I might not see him one last time. It starts with a whim, a pure desire for sex, for one night, and ends with blank, speechless pain.

Friday 6

9:00 a.m. Another vacant day to be got through, and it's all my fault because I lacked the strength to break things off in time, and I accepted the "master's prerogative," in the absolute (that is, he drops by when he wants, phones when he wants), and in short there can be no happiness when one is in a state of oppression. I wonder if his departure might in fact be liberating for me. "When no hope remains, etc.—That is the dawn . . ." But as long as I have the faintest hope of seeing him again (how closely this resembles '58 and my wanting to see CG one more time— and, in the end, he didn't come to say goodbye in my room, where I waited until daybreak), I will remain in this state of ruin.

Monday 9

A call at 6:30 p.m. yesterday. Immediate fatigue. As if all the anxiety and pain built up over the past ten days were subsiding and the work of regaining my calm exhausted me. So, Wednesday afternoon. Probably our last meeting. I'd like to make the next two days stand still because this time I'm waiting for is that of *never again*. It's the soldier's departure for the front . . . the adieux of lovers whom everything conspires to keep apart . . . How will I get through this? Will I be capable of desire on Wednesday?

Tuesday 10

Evening. I think tomorrow will be the last time. It will be a year since the first time he came back with me from Paris, to this house. I'm crying now. A year! I've lived out this passion for a year and done nothing else. The summer, as of mid-July, was entirely devoted to *living* this passion through to the end. Again, with horror, I ask myself: "What is the present?" It undoubtedly exists, it is swollen with the future and with horror: the happiness of seeing him and the pain of not seeing him again, after the three or four hours of our meeting have passed. A silly song plays in my head, *un au revoir, ce n'est pas un adieu . . . Pourquoi ces larmes dans vos jolis yeux . . .* * Goodbye is *always* farewell, since a person usually doesn't know which it will be ahead of time. Just one more meeting, Mr. Executioner . . .

Wednesday 11

4:00 a.m. The countdown will soon begin. I prepared a real celebration, with champagne, a log fire, and a parting gift: an old

---

* Goodbye is not farewell . . . Why are those tears in your pretty eyes? From *Pourquoi Ces Larmes?*, Tino Rossi.

engraving of the Moulin de la Galette. The only way to end things without too much suffering is to *make* the farewell a ceremony.

Thursday 12

We have a little longer . . . He doesn't leave until after the commemoration of the Russian Revolution.

A descent into sadomasochism, but gentle, without violence (because of the combination of sodomy and "normal" sex—bruised all over, at one point, I thought I was torn). He said, "Annie, I love you," and I didn't attach much importance to it because it was during sex, but perhaps that is precisely where the truth, the only truth, resides: in desire. Was afraid, this morning, that his wife may have found strands of hair on him, on the soles of his socks (!), and also that he's had an accident. His life is truly precious to me, and I already ache for Russia, and for what most probably will happen there in the years to come, appalling upheavals. What will become of him?

Retrieved four hairs of his from my comb and immediately thought of Tristan and Isolde: I long to sew his hair into a garment, as Isolde's golden hair was sewn into a dress. *Vivere una favola* . . . When he arrived, we made love on the carpet in the study. Undressing each other is more and more wonderful. When it's time for him to leave, I dress him again (his cuffs need buttoning), and there is so much tenderness in the way we kiss each other afterwards. It was a quarter or half past ten when he left. I didn't sleep more than two hours.

He was wearing baggy white Russian briefs with a thick waistband. I identified them immediately with my hands.

Monday 16

Time moves forward and he does not come. A very irritating trip to West Germany. Bremen was pleasant enough—I am rather numb, truth be told. The Frankfurt debate was abhorrent, futile (of course, I was sure that it would be), and I was attacked by a poet with an axe to grind. I've forgotten his name.

Perhaps he's not coming back because he's afraid I'll give him another present. "Merde!" he said when I said, "I have a present for you"— it was an evening free of taboos of any kind . . . Or maybe he's ashamed of our torrid way of making love, the unbridled pleasure. Or his car has broken down, or . . . Or things I can't think about without quaking with fear—another woman, etc.

In the midst of the wonderful autumn sun, the resplendent trees, I think of last year. I wanted to make this passion a work of art in my life, or rather this affair became a passion because I wanted it to be a work of art (Michel Foucault: the highest good is to make one's life a work of art).

Wednesday 18

An empty day, and tonight I'm crying because it's been exactly one week, and soon there'll be nothing more to hope for. The days cancel themselves out, one by one, and still he doesn't come. A phone call at 1:00 p.m. When I answer, there's no one on the line. It was not, as I had thought, Franke Rother, the East German woman, who arrived in Cergy two hours late, after I had ceased to expect her.

To have spent this late afternoon with her, all dressed up, perfectly coiffed, etc., threw me into despair, *by contrast with* last Wednesday. To say nothing of last year, on the same date . . . The greatest, most extraordinary joy would be for him to appear unannounced one evening. There is not much "extraordinary" left in our relationship with the regulated framework of prearranged meetings. But better an arranged meeting (or anything that gives me a chance to see him) than Nothing.

Thursday 19

At ten to nine: "Annie." In three quarters of an hour he'll be here. After the phone call, I jumped for joy, danced in a way I haven't done since childhood, before the stickiness and shame of adolescence, the *restraint* of the girl student. This joy must be prodigious indeed to be able to restore that of childhood or maybe even that of *before '52*.

Evening. Again the whole bottle of champagne, a little less whiskey for him than last time. The continual invention of positions and caresses. I spill champagne on his penis, quite sure that no one's ever done anything like that to him. Anal sex. Hold on to the memory of his face, his troubled look when I tell him, "Anywhere, anytime, ask me anything, and I'll give it to you, I'll do it for you." There are almost tears in his eyes. I take a piece of something he's eating into my own mouth, he is moved.

Maybe one more time, just one . . . I can't remember all of it, the tenderness, the indistinct words, or each concrete sign

- 179 -

of that tenderness. The amazingly acrobatic position on the leather armchair, upside down. I have an inventive, perfectionist side—its current domain of expression (for the little time that remains) is love.

Saturday 21

I come back from Rouen, where the high point of the day was learning, thirty years after the fact, that the supervisor in chief of the lycée, the terrible R, and the sly Miss F, the headmistress, were a lesbian couple.

I live in terror of this countdown, which will end with the October Revolution. Curiously, as a preventive buffer against pain, I view S in the way I did Ph when I left him (before I went on to marry him), with a brotherly affection, and as someone from whom nothing could separate me.

Bought a black knit outfit, superb. To be the most beautiful of all, for him, at the embassy. I think of last year, walking in the streets of La Rochelle in the morning, going into the Printemps, being on the gray street where the hotel was, strolling in Marseille, entering that open-air café, and it seems like only yesterday, *vchera*.

Monday 23

There was a call, which Éric answered, while I was in Paris. I'm sure that the stranger who hung up was S. I am sick at heart. It's always a mistake to want to meet people like Gérard G, who is unconscious of his ambiguous stance: how he hates the Parisian milieu for rejecting him, and at the same time yearns to be part of it again. Meanwhile I missed S, who may have been able to come today. For days I've had a headache that will not let up. And tomorrow morning, if I'm not here, will I miss S again? How am I going to live without hope, without waiting? There's no longer any resemblance between the man I met in the USSR—callow, very much the apparatchik, lacking in character—and the one whose body is inside me, and whose existence is more dear to me than anything.

Rue Saint-Denis: the clammy heat and insistence of sex, everywhere: in shop windows (aphrodisiacs, latex, leather, etc.) and in the eyes of men. Walking, I keep my eyes lowered, like an attendant in a church, but I'd like to enter these places and see the true face of male desire. A young guy with an attaché case goes in to watch a peepshow (twenty francs) at a place that also shows videos.

Tuesday 24

Received an invitation for the anniversary of the October Revolution, November 6. I'm happy because it means an extension of the deadline: we have at least until Monday. (I thought the party would be on Friday, like last year.) I think of Proust's words about that extra time a soldier imagines being granted in relation to the death that hovers around him. There's the constant hope of a new extension of the deadline, whereas everything must end one day for every human being.

Found the recipe for the celery appetizer, which I thought I'd thrown away. I kept it for twenty years but never made it because no one liked celery. But S likes celery. It's as if I'd kept this recipe all this time just for him.

The weather is splendid, as in '63, in '85, and last year. I don't want to work in the garden because I can't help *thinking* (what if he has someone else? or what if at this moment, he's in the forest of Fontainebleau?). At this moment, I'm extremely unhappy, from waiting, desire and fear. And nothing I do in the garden has anything to do with him. Worse, these flowers will still bloom long after we've separated.

Dreamt of my mother, alive, at the hospice or the geriatric unit of the hospital.

Wednesday 25

This weather . . . this weather . . . I'm talking about the October sun. All afternoon, in the garden, I'm haunted by the same fears, always: 1) that he has someone else, and then I fall into the hole, stuck at a stage of childhood I'll never get past. I read in an article on psychoanalysis about how an infant gradually overcomes *nameless terror* (how I love those words), the terror of separation from the mother. A crucial stage has been reached when the child becomes able to retain an image of the mother when she's not there: in other words, when the child understands that they don't need to physically be together to keep on thinking of each other. Not only does S cease to think of me as soon as he leaves, but he thinks of another woman . . . I'm still in a state of nameless terror . . . 2) that there's a film at the embassy tomorrow and he has willfully neglected to invite me—that he has gone to see Sa or S—that he no longer has the use of a car in which to come to see me (this is a new one, but it has happened *before* . . .)

I received a very beautiful bouquet from the Cergy Saint-Christophe library. I am briefly happy with this reward, then even unhappier than before: the things others give me make me think of what S doesn't give me, his desire and his love.

Thursday 26

10:45 a.m. Less and less hope for the days to come. A feeling of horror, weeping. What if he has left? I still live in fear, after the unidentified phone call on Monday (announcing a sudden departure?).

2:45 p.m. For the first time, I dare to phone the Soviet Embassy so I'll *know* (*knowing, knowing* is the thing . . .) whether or not there's a film today. The answer is *no*, which brings me a little relief—just from my jealousy, not from my desire to see him.

10:25 a.m. Last year, I wrote, "October 26, a perfect day." Today is so dark (but did I plan to keep him for a year?). There were four phone calls, four hopes that died.

Friday 27

I started two books, ten years apart, on October 27 (in '62 and '72). Not this year. During the night, 3:00 a.m., I wept my heart out (I can do that because I'm alone, the boys aren't here anymore). I was sure he had left. This morning, I think it's possible he has. I'll call the embassy this afternoon, maybe. The other facet of my dread is a memory of the woman "who'd worked with Alain Delon"—did S see her again? Monday's phone call worries me more and more. The darkness is the same as in March, and in May, and September, when I returned from Italy. Yet each of these times, I've been convinced I've never felt so low. To remember similar states of mind is of no help at all, and even makes things worse. It confirms the existence of an unchanging misery that has to do with love (no matter what kind of love, or who the recipient is).

Monday 30

3:15 p.m. A frenzy of anxiety and fatalism: "he's gone" or "he's got someone else, he's in a hurry to love before he leaves." It is infinitely difficult. The fine weather has returned—a relentless summer. I'm always on the verge of tears. Such *nameless terror*. Anything that speaks to me of the USSR (and so many things do) rends my heart. Very violent headaches. I dare not think about the state I'll be in if I've had no word from him by Friday. Calling the embassy would be the end of all hope. So don't do it.

Tuesday 31

I think the worst has happened. I have wept my heart out. He has most certainly returned to the USSR. Last Wednesday, when I received the flowers from the library, for a few seconds I thought they were from him, and that he'd left France. It was probably true (that he had left). So he didn't want to say goodbye to me. When I'm certain of it (I'm going to have to call the embassy), how will I keep on living.

Twenty to eleven in the morning. He called. But he cannot come. And naturally, I think of the other possibility—a mistress, another desire. What could be more natural. Monday will be an ordeal. I really feel it. But at least there is something to be *gained*. I'm coming out of darkness.

November
Wednesday 1st

This time, there'll be no extension of the deadline: it really is in November that he's going back to the USSR. There'll be *one* more time, I imagine, and nothing after. Last night's phone call, because he didn't schedule a meeting, did not appease me. I remain in hell. Formless jealousy, fear of Monday, anger at the smooth wall he is, anger at my own weakness and inertia. Time stands still—today is *only* Wednesday.

For five years, I've ceased to experience with shame what can be experienced with pleasure and triumph (sexuality, jealousy, class differences). Shame spreads over everything, prevents any further progress.

I also thought that writing acted as a kind of morality for me. That is why I didn't want to have affairs before, so I wouldn't lose the obsession with writing. For a long time, a life of pleasure seemed impossible to me (it even does now) *because* I write. I forgave my husband's pleasure seeking *because* he didn't write. What else is there to do when you don't write? Eat, drink, and make love.

Thursday 2

Time has never moved so slowly nor been so devoid of future. I'm afraid of Monday, of seeing him attracted to other women, as in May and September (even if I was wrong about that, at least in May), afraid of seeing people I know, see them read on my face and body: "she's not working, she doesn't write anymore." But that's not true, I'm the only one to know—I no longer live in their world of glory or suffering through writing, but in the world of flesh, pain, and desire for a man.

I watched a show on "love and sex" where men were speaking candidly. Based on what they said, I tried to decode the behavior of S—whether he has other women, etc. Absurd, of course. But I seek and seize all the *keys* to knowing . . .

Friday 3

I've really said goodbye to the dream of an intelligent, "solid" (etc.) man with whom I could "build" (?) something. Outside of writing and children, I'm incapable of building anything. My only reality is the temporary man with nothing to offer but dreams and fantasies, along with desire and tenderness, if he's up to it.

When I think that I started to learn Russian for a man!

Continually, in flashes, I imagine a terrible scene of pain and humiliation on Monday at the embassy: "another woman" courted right in front of me. I even catch that murmured phrase, "see you later this afternoon," heard so many times, in that same place, but no longer meant for me. What, then, would be the point of all the finery, painstakingly planned, the black suit which gives me a model's silhouette, the border of black lace, the dark silky stockings, the Charles Jourdan bag and the honey tint which the colorist at Dessange got just right? What's the point if not to prove how inane it all is, in the event of his feeling desire for another woman? It is basically very moral. Will I manage to be dignified and not run away (as I always want to do: in the past, I used to want to slap, to beat the man who'd forgotten me—same thing as running away).

Sunday 5

Cool, gray weather, after two days of rain. Last night, a dream about S: he's invited me to Lille (?), we're in a room, we go out in the street and he makes love to me against a wall and disappears. I realize that I'm just below the apartment of Christiane B and it's the middle of the day. (CB, who can't find a man: the dream is a sign of my age, which is only less than hers by four or five years.) I go looking for S, don't find him. Had another dream, a week ago, that he came to see me with a *blue letter*.

Today, I really feel time *counting down* to the reception tomorrow: sweeping me toward the truth, which I will read in his words and his behavior, without my being able to resist. That old waking nightmare: forgetting the time or the day of some event—realizing it's *too late*.

Monday 6

10:40 a.m. I'm leaving for the embassy soon. Mystery, anguish. My image in the mirror is of little reassurance: makeup applied with almost microscopic precision, the black suit that everyone says looks wonderful on me. But what does it matter if he no longer desires me? . . . Don't speak of love. To advance and conquer, in the emotional arena, is something I've never known how to do.

7:50 p.m. Arriving at the embassy, I had the feeling he wasn't there. He is there, but distracted: "See you this afternoon?" I'm outside of my body, my being. He arrives at four twenty and leaves before eight. The time passed slowly. He didn't say much, I didn't know why. In his mind he's already gone, simple as that. I wept on his shoulder, in his arms. He had bad breath for the first time, and I felt that he was troubled, moved. But maybe it wasn't that at all, he was just in a hurry to leave. The emptiness of it lands on me all at once, the dream of days gone by. I'll probably never see him again, although he only leaves on the fifteenth. But I cling to this tiny hope. The day when I consign to the dirty laundry my two pairs of sperm-soaked underwear from this evening, I will probably be cured.

Scant, almost nonexistent consolation: he thought I looked beautiful at the embassy. What's the meaning of it all, this year of mad love? We made love on my desk (it's me who wanted it), for the first and last time. At the newsstand in the Charles de Gaulle metro, a woman asked me for money. I gave her ten francs, and she kissed my hand, a dreadful sensation (I think of S—that humiliating gesture is like a blessing, it revolts me). Tonight there was a huge black spider in my office. I remember the night in Yvetot, in September '63, the enormous spider my father didn't want to kill ("it's good luck"), and nor did I (I thought of Philippe), and my mother laughed and said, "You two are superstitious!" I didn't kill it tonight, either.

He wore a Guy Laroche tie and a "pocket square," as he calls it. Strange underpants, with a pouch in front, yet "French" so he claimed. He also says, "Such is life. What can you do?" My own words from a year ago. Again he made that gesture of twisting my nose, as if I were a little girl, when I talked to him about the women he's had in France. A confession? Or is he embarrassed that this is not the case? And what does it matter now anyway.

Tuesday 7

Jealousy, right to the end. I attribute his distraction yesterday to his having another woman, just as I do the fact that he didn't come round during the week of brilliant weather in October. Cold and foggy since the beginning of November. He leaves on the fifteenth: just a year after the crazy night when his car wouldn't start.

I haven't slept, cried my eyes out. There remains that sliver of hope of seeing him again, just a sliver. Yesterday on the couch,

I watched him above me, a perfect fit with my body, tall and slender, skin white and smooth: a physical double. The pain more intense because of it. The parting kisses, by the door, are death. His hunched shadow moving toward the car, his dark blue suit. He blows me a kiss. A final image. From my office, I hear the car drive away.

"I'll be back."—"I'll be old."—"You'll never be old for me."—"I'll try not to get old."

Why believe that I suffer more because I "am" a writer? (It's not that *I am* a writer—I write, and I live.)

Thursday 9

Dream: a reception at the embassy (which is very white, and a little antiquated). I am with S, but at one point the Soviets are separated from the guests. I go, leaving him behind. He's listening to Gorbachev, whom I do not see. I arrive at a bridge. Halfway across I decide to go back in order to be with him again. Then I give up and resume my journey, thinking that I'll never see him again.

Deep down, I really don't have any hope of seeing him before he leaves. Monday was too much a farewell scene, and that's the way he took it (even blowing me a kiss as he left). All I can hope for is a phone call. I'm entering a state of suffering, seeking to forget in order to survive.

A book that could start with "From such-and-such a date to such-and-such a date, my life was given over to a passionate affair," etc. Describe it in minute detail. Which means giving up seeing S for good, and maybe causing him harm. On its own, it's quite a limited project anyway.

I can see despair ahead, based on the belief that no book will be able to help me understand what I'm going through—and more than anything, the belief that I, personally, cannot write such a book.

Friday 10

"In the place that is my home, love does not exist but at the cost of death." —Christa Wolf, *No Place on Earth*.

She also says: "Sometimes I think that to sustain me, I would need all the rest of humanity." That is why I write, out of the same lack. This morning, I sank back into a state of suffering and obsession. Lost time has no more meaning in that state because time itself stops. I am in pain because I've started to hope again and therefore to wait for a sign, which is very unlikely to materialize. And also because the last weeks have not gone the way I'd imagined, because he did not come, despite his promises that he would.

Saturday 11

The Berlin Wall has fallen. History again becomes unpredictable. Everything came from the East, and in particular from the USSR, that country that has *hovered over me* for more than a year, as a matter of chance (but because I write, I was

fated to encounter Eastern Europe—Bulgaria, on my first trip).
A sense of encroaching chaos, and reaction from Russia cannot
be ruled out. S will be part of that, obviously, his father having
been decorated by Stalin! I fear the reunification of Germany
(again, a fear determined by the past), as if it could bring on a
third world war. Coincidence: today is November 11.

A problem with the rights to my books, yesterday, swept aside
my suffering over S. Today, though unrelated, the two sources
of anxiety merge. And more and more, the wealth of sensation and life that my passion brings me is forced to fade and
make way for a fact I had to face, sooner or later: that of having
wasted my time on a man who must have been unfaithful to
me several times, and only saw me as a good deal—sex and
fame. Dreamt of him again, in the kitchen: he tells me that he's
never loved anyone but Masha, his wife. Sometimes, in spite
of everything, I have the intuition that things aren't over yet,
and we'll meet again in circumstances that are impossible to
imagine, given the current state of his situation and that of the
USSR. Obstinately keep on learning Russian.

Monday 13

2:00 p.m. The interminable summer of '89, which has lasted
into November. "The end of a dream"—words from a pho-
to-romance novel and the reality they denote—excruciating.
Go back in time to Zagorsk, to the exact moment when I'm
about to think of S in that room full of treasure. Erase everything that happened, which kept me obsessed, my mind even
more than my body, for fourteen months. Be reconciled to my

true age and the onset of menopause. See my skirt suits and blouses bought for a man, for what they are: pointless clothes, worn only for the sake of fashion, in other words, for nothing. He'll be here for two more days, but the hope of seeing him again disappeared today, the only possible time. Nothing remains but the final phone call, which is not a sure thing. My drive to go to the depths of suffering and illusion, both at once.

Dreamt that my mother was in the hospital and I had to go see her. The exact dream: I'm in a huge hospital, with a very large and brightly lit hall. It's nighttime. There's a terrible atmosphere of *déjà vécu* (an experience from when, childhood? A memory of the TB pavilion at the hospital in Le Havre, where my uncle was quarantined?). I want go out onto Place d'Italie. But I'm at the "Quentin-Bauchart" station. Why that name, that street where I've been two or three times at most?

Tuesday 14

Still one day. Try not to see the probable truth, augured by his slightly cruel teeth and narrow eyes: I've been nothing but a conquest and an object of pleasure, which I knew in the beginning and then did my utmost to forget. Will it be harder to erase this past year than the eighteen years with my husband? Hatred made things easier then. Now love complicates them.

Evening, 8:00 p.m. It's obvious: he won't even call before he leaves, due to cowardice, most of all. I could certainly blame him for not coming around, especially for not having given me a photo or some kind of keepsake. "It will be a surprise," he said, when I spoke to him about a farewell gift for me. The "surprise" is that there will be no gift, no photo, nothing, not a *single trace* of him. He was wrong to believe that I am absolutely selfless. Still, to endure such great contempt . . . he is Vronski, worse than Vronski. I have sunk to the very bottom of pain, and now of disillusionment too.

The only way to make me forget his cynicism, his lack of elegance, would be for him to call me from Moscow. One might as well hope for snow in the Sahara.

Wednesday 15

Yes, you can count on the worst thing always happening. I'm paying for my weakness, for having been unable to say, "No, we're not seeing each other anymore, we won't see each other again." But there was never a time when I was able to do it. Thick fog. I don't know what time the train leaves to take him back to the Eastern Bloc. I am crying, yet another loss to mourn, but without guilt. It's worse. The thing I've so often feared has happened. Now to live is to write, and I don't know what to write, or where to begin. I wouldn't want to do something narcissistic and narrow.

So *today* is the day. I watch the trees, the sun on the grass (it's half past twelve), something is slipping away right at this moment, impossible to grasp, conveying me from yesterday's possible presence to tomorrow's definite absence. This day is the juncture between past and future. It is like death. (I had the same feeling upon the death of my father and at my mother's death too: I wrote to connect the day when I'd seen her alive with the day she died.)

7:00 p.m. How is it that I can't *believe* he could have left with no goodbye? Maybe there'll be one last extension. Which means I imagine something quite the opposite from what I did before, when I imagined him gone. There's no certainty, in either case (tomorrow morning, I'll call the embassy). Pettily, I count up everything I gave him: a Dupont lighter—a book about Paris—an old engraving—the newspaper from the day of his birth—cartons of Marlboros, and that doesn't include the innumerable bottles of whiskey, a good twenty or so—smoked salmon and champagne from the last few times. He came to Cergy thirty-four times, and five times to the studio in Paris. This accounting is pointless, since neither forty nor one hundred visits would change a thing about today. All that exists is the break, the never-again, and the pain of lucidity. Right now he is most certainly in a train crossing Germany, sitting next to his wife. A westernized, yuppie-style Soviet couple.

Thursday 16

9:30 a.m. This morning, on waking, I feel certain he is truly gone. In this diary I conserve only a narrow margin between yes and no. I'll phone (always living my life as if it were a serial novel).

He left for Moscow last night. You can always count on the worst thing happening. Will I feel *better* indoors than out, as after my mother's death? In any case, I'm going to go out. To relive the story of *Anna Karenina* was really the stupidest thing

I could have done. I don't even have the strength to regret my weakness, still overwhelmed by the pain of longing. "I'm going to put my sperm on your belly," my name whispered with a Russian accent. I pay too dearly for happiness.

8:30 p.m. What does it mean to love a man? His being there, making love with him, dreaming; and he returns and makes love. It's all just waiting.

Just keep going. Business as usual. For two hours, over the phone, I dealt with problems of English translation for *A Woman's Story*. Then I went to Leclerc. The blue sky, the sun-filled trees, the cold, like last year—Tuesdays in November. I take things from the shelves, put them in the cart. Must keep on thinking I'm the same as before, I have to live. Without my list, made several days ago, I couldn't have bought anything at all. Must not listen to tapes of songs I've heard over the past year. I'm in another era. I go to Trois-Fontaines, buy toning lotion, look for a shawl. Act as if nothing has happened. But the difference between the probability and the certainty of his departure, between fiction and truth, is the same as the difference between life and death.

I see the purple bras, the garter belt in the lingerie shop, at the corner across from Auchan. The bank. Women queue ahead of me. Have they known about this for a long time, losing a man, a mad love? ("I love you, Annie—You're beautiful—I'm going to come, Annie.") They grow impatient. I too look at my watch, as a matter of principle. But I'm only using up time, excess time. Nothing lies ahead of me.

I pass the garter belts again—all that sweetness of lingerie. I go back home, drop off the shopping, phone the CNED.* I go out again, this time to the Catholic Relief thrift shop. Among the scarves and shoes that I leave with them are the slippers I bought for S to wear around the house. An unemployed person will sink his feet in the black leather—I would like them to bring him luck. At Catholic Relief: a busyness and roughness of gesture that I'd forgotten. Men and women—young—try on clothes, shouting to each other. Invisible poverty gathered there.

At the hairdresser's. Music. I don't look at myself too closely, my naked face and wet hair: *age*. Magazines with alluring women, undressed. All this time, walking, driving, I have the sense that I'm continuing to write and live out my *beautiful* love story. I see the tower blocks of the New Town, the express-ways. It's as if I've always been there. My life preceding it is absent.

It is like the days after my abortion, in '64. And now I feel like sleeping.

Phoned Nicole. Me: He's a bastard! She: No, he's unhappy, he preferred not to call. I resent her for presenting me with a version of the story that could take away my anger and foist an ounce of insane hope on me. Such an unlikely version, what's more.

I'm superstitious: maybe I shouldn't have given away his slippers, as if it could cause him to die. The idea is atrocious. Did I love him that much?

In a month, in a year [. . .] Without Titus ever seeing Berenice.

---

* Centre national d'enseignement à distance (National Center for Learning by Correspondence), the author's employer at the time.

10:00 p.m. There was a phone call earlier. A second call made me think it had to be him. It was Éric. I'm unable to believe the absence is real, especially because presence turned into absence without any tangible sign from him (it was the same with my mother's sudden death—but I could recall her body in the morgue). I can understand families of the missing never believing they're dead.

Friday 17

A bleak awakening during the night. Vain efforts to avoid thinking of him. The immediate desire to have myself screened for AIDS. Like a desire for death, and love: "at least he'll have left me that."

To embrace all of life, as I've always done, is so hard, much more than protecting oneself in order to retain the power to write. (But then what is there to write that is true and fair?)

Between ten and eleven, I take down the addresses of psychics from the Minitel. Then I give up. I don't want *predictions* because naturally, I won't be able to forget what is said. I wouldn't be able to keep myself from *believing* it. Minitel's stupid horoscope for this week was enough to bring me back to earth with a bang.

Dreamt about a very beautiful black cat sitting on top of my writing, and something else I don't remember now. Yes, I do: in some kind of school, a chapel, as at Saint-Michel d'Yvetot, students who are studying my books tell me that the *passé composé* is obsolete and that a person has to write in the present or the simple past. I answer: "But how do you talk about what you did yesterday? I write in the *passé composé* because people speak in the *passé composé*."

Continued existence is atrocious. Was awakened by a phone call, a wrong number—a woman with a strange accent. Where there is life, there is hope, even of the wildest kind. Dreamt of Nicole and another woman, and my father, who is quite young, and revolted by the books we're reading, sexual and raw. Undoubtedly an Oedipal dream.

My entire problem is not knowing how long this state will last. My only comparison is the death of my mother. It was the book I wrote about her that saved me, and I'm not *allowed* to write about him. But in many ways I'm *reliving* October–November '82—the same conjunction of loss and the book to write.

There are times when my anguish fades. I'm drowsy, as if I hadn't slept since Leningrad. Then this thought recurs, about anything at all: there's no point in cleaning *x*, *y*, or *z*, in buying pistachios, salmon, etc. And: maybe he'll never come back to this study, this bedroom where we so often made love. I'll forget his face. Already there's the white shawl, bought yesterday, which he'll never see. Or else he will come back, never speak of Stalin anymore, have gotten fatter, and drink more whiskey. There'll be little broken blood vessels over his cheekbones. And me? Here's the pledge I made to him: I'll try not to age. I'll always remain at fifty-seven kilos. There are gold thread lifts and other ways of cheating if my wrinkles grow more pronounced. I know he didn't love me as much as I did him, but it is because of him, for him, that I would like to write a very beautiful book.

Sunday 19

Was left with an impression of extreme buffoonery, yesterday, watching a production of *Phèdre* in which all roles were played by one actress (Claude Degliame). This stylized, ultra-choreographed, esthetic representation of the pain of love does not resemble mine. Racine's text on its own, unadorned, is closer.

Dreamt I was getting ready for a trip to Turkey—probably a displacement of my desire for a trip to the USSR. In the dream, I try to resell the pearl necklace that came to me from my ex-husband's grandmother. Then I try to get to a highway, but I go the wrong way several times in a row. I arrive at some railroad tracks, which people are crossing, but it's very dangerous (does this have a connection with the end of *Anna Karenina*?). I turn around and take quite a long detour to get back on the right road (I was able to remember where I'd got onto the *wrong* road). The right road runs below the railway tracks.

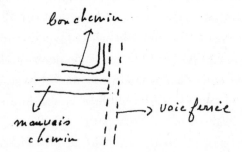

In all this, I've been granted some kind of grace, for I do not dream of S.

I realize with astonishment that I've completely forgotten certain events from '89, for instance, that I went to see plays by Molière at the Cergy theater. Sylvie reminded me of this, and I cannot possibly put a date to those performances. I was playing the role of "extra" in my own life for the entire year.

Like other women, I will calmly do my errands, take an interest in the books and movies coming out, watch flowers break through the soil in January and February. Is this *better* than shopping for clothes, thinking about the caresses of the night before and dreaming of the ones to follow, waiting with your heart in your throat? . . . No, probably not. Otherwise I wouldn't have looked back with longing on Rome and Venice '63 for so many years.

Monday 20

In the morning, I don't want to get up. I remain in bed, curled in a ball, unmoving. Stomach pains. Dismaying perceptions—all the memories that make me think that S was a Don Juan. Those are not the worst. Others: his wish not to leave any trace of himself behind when he left, neither photos nor objects; the fear of people finding out about our affair.

A sense of my own mediocrity, a general lack of courage, particularly when it comes to writing.

Wednesday 22

Last night, images of the Russian–German war in the documentary *From Nuremberg to Nuremberg*. Leningrad, 1941: the heart-stopping courage of the Soviets, their almost mystical resistance. "My father was decorated by Stalin." The pain I feel at having known and lost an entire world, at having glimpsed something I could never have imagined before, because it had never been embodied, in a face, words, a pair of hands: the communist ideal which rallied men and women in Leningrad, in Stalingrad, and was passed on to that blond green-eyed boy, who had no sense of betraying anything or anyone when he yearned for Guy Laroche ties and suits by Saint Laurent.

Friday 24

Eighteen days since I saw him for the last time. Haven't yet surpassed the maximum time, which was twenty-four days in April and September. But there is no more waiting now, counting days makes no sense. One day it will be two, three, six months since I've seen him. One day, as I'm closing the double curtains in my office, I'll no longer think, as I do every night now, that the last time we met he'd wanted to close them himself. Me: "It's tricky." Him: "I can do it."

Dreamt of a trip by car. There is Irène S (always signifying the USSR), and a dog (because of the Children's Book Prize awarded to Nadja's *Chien bleu*?). Yet I'm alive. I sometimes think I'd be able to sleep with another man (without knowing, or wanting to know, my deep-seated motives for doing so:

pain, the certainty of never seeing S again, the fear of aging, the desire for a man, habitual and self-regenerating).

More and more I have the dark feeling—or not even dark, just saddening—that it was out of indifference that he neglected to call me before leaving, and above all so as not to have to contend with my request: what will you give me to remember you by (the photo I repeatedly asked him for)?

Sunday 26

Another dream, this time of our reuniting in Moscow, more beautiful than if it were to happen in France. Behind the dream is a sense that this will never happen, an intuition whose strength I perceive in the fact that I'm working very hard on my writing project and don't really *want* to travel to Moscow, which would cost me time. Because for S, I was only a gratifying affair, whose ending was decided long ago, and which survived. Maybe the desire to write, to *do*, compels me to prefer this hopeless version of the story.

Monday 27

Three weeks. I am now in a state of sorrow, not pain. Sorrow about the lack of hope, the work I have to do, and time, which only ages me, with no pleasure in exchange. Racing heart and revulsion in the mornings. Many dreams, one about a visit from my former in-laws. In the dream, I'm still married and am hosting Maurice, his wife, Pierre, and my mother-in-law.

I'm afraid of having aged, as it's been a long time since I last saw them. I realize that my clothes are horrible, a fusty pink sweater, etc. A scene with my husband: I refuse to make green beans unless everyone helps to prepare them—all my resentment as a housewife, summarized. Pain upon awakening, to think of all that time lost with my husband, eighteen years . . .

Tuesday 28

As always, I wake to a day with no hope. I hear a song that used to leave me cold, *Oui, c'est moi, Jérôme, non je n'ai pas changé / Je suis toujours celui qui t'a aimée.** (Who sang it? Claude François?) I cry into my breakfast because it talks about a man returning. Now, in my mind, I almost always picture S as tall, gentle, and naked, the image of him I've kept from our meetings. I don't think he has forgotten everything, the erotic splendor of certain days. But that's of no comfort at all, quite the opposite: all thought leads to the absence that is memory. The only moment, lately, when I've had a positive reaction, I saw myself as still sexy (literally a turn-on for the photographer yesterday), the way I appeared to S when he left me, in the black outfit that because of him I'd like to wear all the time. I thought of myself at sixteen, in April '57, when the postman gave me a letter from G de V in the street: wild happiness and yet I never saw G de V again. (Symmetry between this letter and a "sign" from S, which someone at the Soviet film could give me, day after tomorrow, but no one will.)

---

* Yes, it's me, Jerome, no I haven't changed / I'm still the guy who loved you.

December
Friday 1st

Today marks the first whole month of no hope. I went to see *Zerograd* at the Soviet embassy. I am in a *blank* state, devoid of pain and nostalgia. For the first time, I actually follow the movie. To state the obvious: if he didn't say goodbye it was to avoid any kind of request from me, and because for him I was already just a memory (a pleasant one, I think). I'm an empty space. If he gives no sign of life, how can I wait for him? I yearn for a little affair, a distraction, nothing more, as a way of forgetting (the purchase of condoms is symptomatic). I dreamt of postcards written to refuse a request for a meeting (with whom?), in three attempts. One card is too brief, abrupt. The second cites my mother's death as an excuse and the third "the mourning of a family member," although I don't much like to write that, out of superstition. They relate to my lack of resolution about my book.

Saturday 2

I should not reread this journal, it is sheer horror. The written pain, the waiting, was always hope, always life. (I am crying.) Now even that pain is no longer possible. Only emptiness awaits me. *Nameless terror* or emptiness, what a choice!

Sunday 3

Tormented dreams. I'm having an affair with a young man. I'm jealous, I leave him on a road, and immediately see him walk away arm-in-arm with a girl—red jacket, blue skirt. Bitterness. Every morning, it's hard to get out of bed. I have to relearn how to forget. All the couples I see kissing wrench my heart. The only thing I see in our story now is an affair with an apparatchik who was very much in love with me for a month or two, before habit set in, and whose sole concern was that no one know about it, on account of his career. What would be the point in looking for other "signs" of this truth, set down in this journal as early as October? The total silence he'll maintain forever, or for years, more surely than anything else, will bring me to the point of forgetting—my only consolation.

The Malta summit. In five years, what will have become of the Eastern Bloc? East and West Germany united? The USSR, the USSR . . . How can one help wanting, in both head and heart, to be in that country, in Moscow? That cry of "To Moscow!" which people would shout at communists. The play on words, *Moscou pas comme ça* (don't shake me up like that).*

Wednesday 6

The Parti Communiste de France and its suffocating love of writers. An encirclement strategy and then, socially, you surely die in becoming "the communist writer." I only like the USSR and not the PCF, of course. It's been exactly one month since the last time I saw S. The way he left without saying goodbye foretold the future: no more signs of life before a (hypothetical) return to the West. In any case, he couldn't call me unless

---

* *Ne me secoue pas comme ça.*

he were *victorious* (having landed some prestigious position or another).

Thursday 7

Dreamt I was going to spend Christmas in the USSR, in a small town I cannot locate. This is related to an invitation from the Maison des Écrivains to go spend six months in . . . Dieppe! I have the address of the VAAP in Moscow, but pride, or clarity of vision, has made me decide against sending S a book for Christmas through this channel. Best to be forgotten and not create the impression that I can get hold of S against his will. He's a good friend of Chetverikov, the president of the VAAP, a diplomat dismissed by Mitterrand in '83 on suspicion of being a member of the KGB. S himself wasn't with the KGB, it seemed to me (lack of evidence goes with the territory). How often might I have explained in terms of affairs with other women things which were, in fact, connected to the (always secret) politico-diplomatic context of the Soviet Union? My only true rival was his "career," a position so difficult to keep in these times of perestroika.

Saturday 9

A dream of snow in the garden (maybe because yesterday I learned to say in Russian "the earth is covered with snow"— *sneg*), of children in a tree (what were they doing there?), and I have to go down to a garage through the basement (ours is an exterior garage). I hardly remember my dreams if I don't force myself to memorize them on waking. All that remains is snow falling from the fir trees in clumps. Disturbing.

Tuesday 12

When will mornings cease to be the way they are now, sheer desperation? Yet before I get up, I'm able to imagine his body and face with the utmost precision, without suffering or desire: he was right *there*, completely *there*, with his unreadable, deep-set eyes, his neck, his hair, the curve of his shoulders, his sex, wrists, and powerful hands. One day I won't be able to perform this operation of memory in such complete and perfect detail. I can even feel the texture of his skin, taste his sex, his mouth. It upsets me to write it down, whereas this morning I could think of it without pain.

How much time each morning will I continue to *sacrifice* to my passion, that is, be unable to start the day without pain?

Thursday 14

S returns constantly, in waves, sudden tears—it's still very difficult, one month later. Of course there is no hope, and yet writing this means I do hope, quite madly (although reason and observation of the last months of our relationship make it clear that his departure should have marked the precise moment of its ending). When he has a new position, stable and preferably an improvement over the last one, he may think of calling.

Friday 15

For almost a month, my view of what I meant to him has grown increasingly bleak. It's always the same story: knowing, *deep inside*, what the truth is, even writing it down here, while at the same time not believing, rejecting it. Scenes come back to me now which, over the course of the year, briefly sounded the alarm: his face and smile at the Hotel Rossia on that first day, when I sensed he wanted to kiss me, though he didn't know me—therefore, a real womanizer . . . and at the France–USSR event in November '88, when he left with a bunch of girls from the embassy, that look of falsity on his face.

More and more trouble sleeping. Dreams: a Russian train, which "one can get off of" but only "at the risk of one's life." I find S there, naked. But nothing happens. It doesn't last long, or I wake up. Also dreamt of a play, of which I read a very bad review. It's adapted from a text about an adolescent, published in *Je bouquine*.* In my dream, the title is very clear.

Wednesday 20

Irritating weekend and Monday. Frustration, and most of all the sense of being a complete nonentity. DS is in Moscow, moreover giving her usual speech on threatened "values," the role of intellectuals, etc., a speech I've told myself I will reply to. But I'm not doing it. She'll probably be chosen as a juror for the Prix Renaudot. Even though I didn't really want to be

---

* A cultural magazine for twelve- to fifteen-year-olds, devoted to literature for teens. Created in 1984, part of the Groupe Bayard Presse.

chosen, and know it's better for me not to be chosen, the old jealousy of the only child crops up again.

Dreamt of S and his wife, he is reckless in his displays of intimacy with me.

I'm tired, my arms and ribs hurt (from carrying a too-heavy carpet), and I'm still unsure of the *path* my book is taking.

My suffering over S lurks just beneath the surface. To reread a page of this journal from October, November, makes me weep with pain. I am below literature right now. I hope, believe it's *possible* that he'll send me New Year's greetings, without including his address, and in my head I compose an answer to a letter not yet received.

Thursday 21

I dream of S in Yvetot: breakfast in the kitchen. I make him bread and jam and ask if his wife does the same (she does). I kiss and caress him, he wants me, and we go up to my room. My mother is in the "little bedroom" at the top of the stairs, washing herself. S is annoyed. He must pass right in front of her to follow me to my room. It's always that setting. A difficult waking, of course.

Friday 22

I sleep poorly. I don't want to do anything. Morning: the world is pointless, I have trouble writing. At times, certain memories of S seem very close, as do things that happened in the same period: the earthquake in Armenia, Micheline V's visit to my house in November or December '88. But when I "review" July–August '88, lunch with Christiane B, Annie M, or the writing of my entry for Garcin's *Dictionnaire,** I feel how much time has passed.

Thursday 28

I'm beneath everything, even remembering. S is reduced to a trail of suffering, the pain of his final disappearance. Everything fills me with horror: the future courses to prepare for Vanves, the prospect of writing. Nothing lies ahead. The Christmas holidays are horrible. I have a dream about Romania, as if a kind of nightmare-Europe had begun there. It is '78–'80 taking hold of me again, but differently from then. I don't have to free myself from anything now. And I'd rather change the order of the world than change my desires; that says it all. It's pointless desire, however, so very pointless. I've even stopped believing I'll get a card from him.

There's been no joy in my life since November 15. There's no bright promise up ahead. I want to sleep all the time, after nights of insomnia. I cannot *believe* he left without saying goodbye. "Take no action. Expect nothing." I was searching my mind for the name of the play those lines are from. They're not from a play, but the Tarot. I don't know which card—the Tower, I think.

---

* Dictionary of contemporary French literature whose first edition was begun in the late '80s, under the direction of the journalist Jérome Garcin, and published in 1989. Each writer was asked to write a note about themselves in the form of an obituary.

At the same time, I long to have a different life, to travel, meet people, dive into the "real" world, not the one in which I spend most of my time, the one made of nothing but words. As in Yvetot in the old days, I don't want to "grow old in this bedroom." Today, the room is not a bedroom, but a study overlooking a garden.

Saturday 30

Mist reminiscent of the last months of '79, ten years ago. My mother was in hospital, and the year that followed left only flat memories: lacking relief, not to say sad and full of boredom (the trip to Spain). Dreamt the other day of the paving stone from Leningrad, collected last year from the banks of the Neva. Souvenir of the USSR . . .

I file and discard papers concerning my mother and see how obsessed, how affected I was by her final years, her death. I never remember the pain of the past, which means that I always experience new pain as a kind of abandonment. Likewise, nothing I do appears to me good or beautiful, except when it is past. My October text on Québec seems good to me, and I believe myself incapable of producing another of comparable quality right now.

I feel I'm at a turning point, but of what, I don't know.

Sunday 31

Dreamt of an old woman. I'm looking for a room in a pastry shop. I'm directed toward another house where I will find one by passing through a tiny street. It's a dead-end street, with brooms and backyard objects. I leave again by car. A huge tire rolls across the square, I am not hit. Dreams related to my difficult life.

Everything I wished for on January 1, 1989, more or less came true, except I didn't know the price I'd have to pay.

1990

January
Monday 1st

Will 1990 change my life, as '60 and '70 did—and '80, to a lesser degree (though my divorce was in the works, inside me)? To ask myself the question is to express the desire that it will. But the unknown, uncontrollable upheaval does not inspire me overmuch.

Wishes which, if they come true, will be enough to make me think myself fulfilled: the first (because I can't really live without it), in January, commit myself to a book, one I've started to write, or another, after giving it some thought. The second wish is to hear from S, *in January*, and see him again in 1990, in the East or the West. Really, the greatest joy of all would be a conjunction of love and History, a Soviet (r)evolution in which we could meet again, à la *Gone with the Wind*—the book which, without my knowing, forever shaped my view of emotions by the age of ten. It is such a beautiful thing to long for, imagine, that I'm incapable of wishing for a new affair with a man who is neither Russian nor blond with green eyes.

Mist. A family day ahead. How will History evolve over the next ten years? (Before now, people never talked about decades, the horizon has broadened.) In my personal life these are the years when I'll have to *resist* (physical decline) and testify (writing).

I forgot to include my great desire to return to the USSR, on a "mission."

Wednesday 3

Dream: I have to sit for an exam at the same time as my sons. The feeling of not knowing anything. I take my parents' Renault 4-CV. My mother is sitting next to me and I am driving. A policeman blows his whistle, I think I've gone through a red light. But in fact, he doesn't want to let me go through because of the car's poor condition. I'm dismayed because I won't be able to sit for the exam. Questionable interpretation: I wanted to succeed in my studies because of my mother. The law. What else? Is this related to my book, which I am still wavering about?

Sunday 7

Again, what do I do with the memory of so much *beauty*, the word I used on getting home from Moscow in September '88? Tonight I remembered the sari I wore in August. I unfolded it. There are marks on the silk from our lovemaking that day. Pure absence. I have no courage, no desire. The book I want to write does not make its presence felt (that is nothing new), but here there is the *other* story, the real one, still inside of me, of which I cannot speak.

Tuesday 9

Dying of not dying: for the first time I understand the meaning of these words. The only thing that would enable me (at least I think it would, though have no proof) to really work without feeling I have to relearn how to live and work each morning, would be the certainty of seeing S again, therefore, a sign from him.

At the moment, I have a sense of wheeling between endeavors and desires that I cease to find appealing within minutes or days of setting them in motion (books begun, a trip to Abu Dhabi planned).

Wednesday 10

Monday, saw AM. I don't like so-called intellectual conversations, which in fact are so full of ideology and beliefs that they are infinitely more false than simple banter like when you say, "It's hard to leave an apartment where you are happy living," and everything connected to feelings and experience.

Dreamt of a Russian (not S) with whom I'm starting to have a loving relationship (but he looks like him!) and also about Pouilly-sur-Loire. And now it's been over *two months* since S disappeared from my life.

Thursday 11

The weather is nice, and for the first time I can listen to cassettes from the summer again—"La Lambada," "San Francisco," and even "Le bal chez Temporel," while driving in the New Town. I feel how much I loved the world while S was "in my life," as the saying goes. This going back in time doesn't make me suffer. Maybe I've already begun to see things with him the way I did in the beginning: as a beautiful, surprising story, not a painful one. I know those songs will remain linked to him, but in the form to which I'm accustomed, as art: emotion and distance—emotion that is positive because it is distanced.

Saturday 13

Dreamt of a hotel where you have to check out before noon. The cleaning lady forces me to pack my suitcase. It takes a long time to gather everything together. What is the meaning of this suitcase—the recent or more distant past? Before that, a more traumatic dream: I've climbed to the top of I don't know where, and a gun is pointed at me (by whom? my husband?), to kill me. But this is happening in the early '80s (in the dream, I know that I'm *reliving* a past situation, very strange).

Monday 15

Fast-paced, tangled dreams. I am taking courses, as if I needed to do everything again, and pass exams. I see GD again. (Didn't I have a kind of contempt for her, deep down? Such a child-woman!) A clearer dream: at the Ls' villa, which I so admired as a child, on rue du Clos-des-Parts, I eat outside with a girl (who? Lydie?) and my ex-husband, fat and ugly, unrecognizable. A huge truck passes, the driver looks out, stops, and asks me if I recognize him. I don't. It's Dujardin, from Lillebonne. He has recognized me. He's no older than me, his name doesn't ring a bell (this is related to my book). Then there's another house, and the "charming young man," B, and his girlfriend? An erotic atmosphere as we brush against each other. Obviously this is because I still wonder what attracts him, and in August '88, I daydreamed quite a lot about him. But the moment passed, and then there was S. Last Friday, in pain from the stomatology session at the hospital, in order to endure it, I imagined S when I kissed his penis. Thinking, only thinking of it makes me cry in writing this. Even the pain of November, though excruciating, seems preferable now.

Tuesday 16

Since I have nothing more to write in this journal but dreams . . . I'm in some kind of bus, a visit to an ill-defined "educational" setting. I've lost my handbag—how many times have I lost my bag in dreams over the past ten years? An unmistakable sign of unease, worry, not a fear of losing my femininity, as in the psychoanalytical cliché.

If I see S again before July 1, I'll go to Padua. Wishes keep me alive and aren't as dangerous as consulting psychics, who are too real and who speak. Not a word is forgotten. Everything calls for action.

Many dreams, one of which is atrocious. An agitated woman with many children arrives at the bank of a river. She's holding one child at the end of a long rope. This child, who can barely walk, enters the water, the others too. The woman keeps screaming that these children are unbearable. I realize that the child tied to the rope is drowning, and another little girl has been struck with a rock. And (this is the most awful), through the transparent water, we see a child floating. The woman keeps repeating that it's not her fault. I'm afraid this woman represents my mother (I felt that she would let me die) and myself (the fear that my children would die; my abortion).

Another dream takes place in the Soviet Union, in a hotel room. A man enters as if it were his room and comes out again. I'm building up a stock of crêpes, multigrain bread. I have too much. Through binoculars, I watch people dancing or protesting in the street. I dream again, of a house, more beautiful than this one. In one bedroom, there are two windows.

This afternoon I leave for Marseille, as in October '88, but I no longer feel the same desire and suffering. Yesterday, a "posthumous" flash of jealousy: Marie R wants to see me, and I think it's to tell me that she slept with S. Everything would reasonably go to prove the opposite, and yet I'm overwhelmed with pain. February 2, the date on which she seems intent on meeting, makes me very anxious.

Friday 19

On the train back from Marseille I read a passage from Calvino's *If on a Winter's Night a Traveler*, the passage about the "Japanese book on a carpet of leaves," etc., and all at once I'm filled with burning desire, an incredible longing to make love, though since S left, I've been all but frozen. I could weep from the memories, the lack, all the vanished sweetness. To lose a man is to age several years in one fell swoop, grow older by all the time that did not pass when he was there, and the imagined years to come. This desire also means I might be ready to fall back into the same kind of *favola* with someone else.

Wednesday 24

I'll go to the film at the embassy tomorrow and maybe get some news of S. Mad hope springs back to life sometimes— the hope, for example, that he's been transferred somewhere close to France. In that case, I believe he'd call—if not, life and human relations would be really too atrocious. After all, he came here to my home, he sometimes said, "I love you," he desired me, a lot . . . But I "give" him until my trip to Abu Dhabi, and if, after that, he shows no sign of life, forgetting must be forced in one way or another. Because now time is empty, it passes in a vertiginous way. I write more and more slowly, ten lines in two days.

Friday 26

Soviet film at the embassy. No news of S. A film from 1956 about the struggles in a raion of kolkhozes. To understand S would also mean to understand the women in kerchiefs who lived at the same time I was dancing to rock 'n' roll, the communist organization, etc. That place, the embassy, seems—becomes—a little more foreign, a little stranger each time. But last night, I thought again, was still thinking of, his body, his eyes.

Right now, I'm waiting for a professor and journalist, Hélène S. I remember waiting for S in the afternoons—it's agony still, enough to make me weep.

Monday 29

The worst part is continuing to wait when there's no longer anything to wait for. Moreover, I have an insane amount of time on my hands, which I don't do very much with: I'm not sure of having chosen the right path, or rather the right *voice*. And, in addition, there's the fear of running short of money if I don't publish in '91, or in '92 at the latest.

Wednesday 31

Tomorrow is February. At the first and the fifteenth day of each month (like interest arriving in a savings account), I vaguely wait for a sign that S has returned to the West and for him to call me. It will be three months soon. I'm so little healed, and everything is slow and pointless, even writing, though it's not as bad as the rest.

I'm rereading my journal from October–November—how many things I've already forgotten. This phrase by Borges is so beautiful, "Century follows century, and things happen only in the present. There are countless men in the air, on land and at sea, and all that really happens happens to me."* I knew this, with the greatest possible intensity. The present: all last summer, I asked myself, "What is the present?" It is me, me . . . It's been obvious all along.

I am writing from a place struck by horror—June '52.

February
Thursday 1st

Sunshine, everything is blue and gold and sweet. Birds chirp and, abruptly, the sadness of adolescence is upon me. Someday, someone should probably say how close a woman feels to adolescence between the ages of forty-eight and fifty-two. Same expectations, same desires, but you're heading into winter instead of summer. But you "know life!" So little. Just a few small ways of not suffering so much. I'm meeting the "charming young man" tonight, with nothing else in mind than the pleasure—and how—of spending time with quite a pretty boy. I am still completely filled with longing for S, excruciatingly specific.

Friday 2

A day spent in the "literary milieu." A feeling of impurity and

---

* Jorge Luis Borges, *Ficciones*, trans. Anthony Kerrigan (Grove Press, 1962).

disgust whose source is difficult to define. Fawning over Kundera, but these games have an impact on literary history because people, teachers in particular, admire what is presented to them with so much authority and collective endorsement. These games are not innocuous. Writing is definitely a form of morality for me still. I feel strongly that writing and passion, like the one I had with S, are inalienable values, with a notion of *purity* attached to them, and of beauty. Last year I'd forgotten my previous revulsion. I made my way through it all with my passion.

Monday 5

Dreamed of my mother, who was alive and reasonably well in spite of her "illness." She has bought shoes that are a little too delicate, and she can't walk properly in them. She tells a story that she is unable to make coherent. However, her condition is satisfactory, compared to that of my mother-in-law (who really is alive and also has Alzheimer's). Dreams, that dream, give me the feeling that time is reversible. I thought my mother had died but at the same time come to life again, was only sick, and back in the flow of time, indeterminate by definition.

I sleep very badly. In my state of insomnia, through force of will, I *see* S. Last night it was downstairs, from behind, as he adjusted the TV, wearing my dressing gown. I can still imagine his body, feel every inch of his skin. I thought it frightening, and nothing less than madness to really see what you've only seen in imagination up until then. Also thought a great deal about the "charming young man," for the days go by so quickly.

Wednesday 7

Can't get past the pain of mornings—no, I'm not there yet. Dreamt of S, whom I was seeing again—in Poland, I think. I live outside men—I mean, outside the male realm—and it's as if I were completely outside the world. Every day I have to create a schedule all over again, and convince myself to write. The future no longer means anything.

Saturday 10

I convince myself, without too much difficulty, that an affair with B, the "charming young man," would be nice. But it's mostly in my head. He doesn't exist for me, and besides, I rarely desire the same man twice. He doesn't know it, but something could have happened between us in August '88. Just the idea of sending S a card (which he may not even receive), from Abu Dhabi or Dubai, gives me an absurd goal in life. He made me dream and suffer so much that I find it hard to *give him up*, or rather give up the image, the memory of him.

I could only make advances to B if I were drunk.

Monday 12

Françoise Verny, last night on FR3, says that her sole regret is not having accepted me at Grasset (in '74?). On this broadcast of *Le Divan d'Henry Chapier* she quotes only B.-H. Lévy and me (a loathsome rapprochement, but the two names are quite far apart in Verny's remarks. Moreover, she boasts of having discovered B-HL and regrets not having published me—I prefer things that way around). It satisfies the vanity. But F. Verny is very intelligent and the kind of woman whom I greatly respect. On *Apostrophes*, in '88, when everyone was fleeing her (those intellectuals, petty-bourgeois and so squeaky-clean, when it comes right down to it), I felt great fondness for her, drunk and superb. At the same time, when I hear her glowing comments, I feel she must be talking about some other woman, more talented, more everything than me: a sort of ideal, like the voice I once heard through my bedroom window in Lillebonne, not knowing it was the echo of my own voice. And I drag myself beneath that voice belonging to a woman who does not exist, an image to which I aspired and will never measure up.

The sense that I'm going to Abu Dhabi only to send S a "Warm wishes" postcard.

Tonight I saw *Germany, Pale Mother*. I've always suspected that this film would speak to me. It is rare to find truth and beauty in a book or film that takes no account of time and History: changes in humanity, throughout and as a result of History. A superb and terrifying film, which takes its title from a poem by Bertolt Brecht (another wonderful coincidence).

Life and Fate, such a great book, *Germany, Pale Mother*, such a great film. And me—what am I writing?

Thursday 15

Sleeplessness and then vague, menacing dreams. I'm on the Saint-Satur road, but when I reach the bridge, the way is blocked and there's just enough room to turn around, almost flush with the water. I go to a strange café, like a small living room. I meet Annie Leclerc (whom I've never actually seen),* amazed to find her there—"what a coincidence!"—but she leaves a little while later. There's a fire in the bathroom of this house, caused by Éric. I suggest using the fire extinguisher from the kitchen cupboard. It has disappeared, David is suspected. But then I find it again. In another dream, I drive recklessly, but without having an accident. I wake up at seven, thinking I've heard the phone ring. It's impossible to know whether I dreamt it or not. I feel uneasy about all the things I ought to be doing. It is clear that every day I spend away from here (yesterday, in Paris) revives my pain, the sense of lack, and my indifference to writing. And I'm leaving for Abu Dhabi on Sunday . . .

Friday 16

It seems that it was S de Beauvoir's fantasy to have her life, her whole life, recorded on a giant tape recorder. Considering all that she wrote about being and freedom, how strange it is that this woman should have had this desire—so flat and pointless—as if filming, recording, all the acts and words of a lifetime would be revelatory of something, but that's not at all the way things go. To explain a life, you'd also need to have everything that influenced a person, all that they had read; and even then something remains concealed that cannot be exposed.

---

* Annie Leclerc, French writer, 1940–2006, known for her militancy and commitment to the cause of prisoners. Author of *Parole de femme* (1974), an influential text of the French feminist movement of the 1970s.

Saturday 24

Over this past week, fate has decided that I will speak about S de Beauvoir on *Apostrophes*. I immediately accepted, despite the additional delay this will mean for my book. For me it is a "duty," a sort of tribute, or rather repaying a debt. I would probably not be what I am, not entirely, without her, without the image I had of her throughout my youth and my years of education (up to the age of thirty). And that she died eight days after my mother, in '86, must also be a sign. Mingled fear and longing to impart something positive, some idea of the way in which literature works.

What can I say about the Arab Emirates? The joy of travel, of seeing things one has only imagined (in my case always poorly); irritation with the formalistic nature of the activities, etc. But, strangely (and it has been this way for a long time), nothing weighed on me. Impossible to make advances to the guide: he was the spitting image of J. F. Josselin! I preferred to think of the charming young man. However, the first thing I did, on Monday afternoon, in my room (I see myself, seated at the table by the TV, with a lamp to the left, a mirror in front, and the noise of the main avenue which carried all the way up to the thirteenth floor, room 1314), was to send a card to S from Abu Dhabi in care of the Soviet embassy in France. "Very best wishes, from the Persian Gulf, A. Ernaux." Will he receive it? If he does, there are two possible outcomes. A phone call, or silence. The latter could have several meanings: indifference, the refusal to reinitiate contact, even the most distant kind, or happiness at not being forgotten but with no desire for contact. This card was written to elicit a sign of life, either annoyance or remembrance.

The weather is wonderful. Summer has been restored to me—last summer, when I lay in the sun, waiting. I felt that already so much time had passed. The winter without him is coming to an end. It would still—would always—make me very happy to see him again.

March
Friday 2

N's horrifying remark on Wednesday evening: "You don't like to be dominated like other women do?" She meant intellectually. Therein lies the divide between women, the ones for whom this phrase rings true and those for whom it doesn't.

At the Filonov exhibition, there is a recording in which he says, "When you're having difficulty doing something, you have to keep going; it's by discovering the solution that you really do something new."

Last year, at this time, my love story was about to cause me suffering. I have started to forget, but sometimes I imagine us meeting again, and it makes me weep.

For the first time since I've lived in the Paris region, I saw the prunus tree flowering in February (the Japanese quince in January), and the magnolia is about to bloom. There is a profusion of violets. The weather is cold (o degrees), for the first time since December. Is my life "turning"? More in the way of a record turning over than the turning of a page. What I imagine most of all is a sundial.

Tuesday 6

The old songs, *Le printemps sans amour. C'est pas l'prin-temps*—"spring without love is not spring." In spite of my activities, *Apostrophes*, there is the extreme pain of days that are identical by virtue of the question, "how long will I go on without loving a man?" The problem is, I can't go to bed with just anyone. I need to feel desire, real desire, the kind I felt in the streets of Leningrad on that Sunday in September, at Dostoevsky's house, at the ballet, and in that room at the Karelia hotel, with the group. It is all still horribly alive. Nothing about his body has been forgotten. The other night, in a state of utter hopelessness, I gave myself an orgasm (something I almost never do anymore) in order to *be* his orgasm, be him, for a moment. To talk about S de Beauvoir and Sartre will be to talk about S, though there's no comparison, and objectively he's nothing but a Russian apparatchik.

Wednesday 7

The happiness of S de Beauvoir's diary makes me so envious. Rereading my own fills me with horror. It seems that last year, in March, life was nothing but defeat, disgust, and jealousy. Again, this year, my heart sinks to think of this month. But more than anything, I wonder how, by what means, I could find a little *tranquility*. Last year was horror, shapeless sorrow; this year, what is the setting, the solution? Nowhere but in those moments I waited for S, and when he was here and we were making love. Will I ever get over this? From his disappearing without a trace? I'm correcting the English translation of *La place*. The day he left, I was doing the same thing with the English translation of *Une femme*. Four months. I always weep at the memories. Even now, the things I do are for him, and I don't even feel like doing them: a preface about the Tour de France, *Apostrophes*.

Friday 9

This March is not like '86 but is just as "uncertain," my writing interrupted for external reasons—the presentation on S de Beauvoir (I've had more than my fill of her letters to Sartre). Irritation with the book by K, who will also be on *Apostrophes*. In addition, I'm trying to radicalize my work of mourning S: I've stopped studying Russian. B, the charming young man from the summer of '88 (two years ago, soon) is coming around on Thursday evening. Fantasies have taken hold of me again, to the point where I barely sleep from imagining the possibilities, or rather the impossibilities (isn't he just coming over to talk about his "stories," the desire for publication?). I'm very vulnerable, and so physical, which is nothing new, and has become more and more true of me in the past seven years, since I regained my freedom. Relations with him are a weird little business. First we met in Neuilly, then in a café on boulevard Saint-Germain. I saw him twice again in '89, bored, because I'd met S, and then once a month ago at the Pont-Royal, with greater interest, even quite a lot. What will be next? On the phone, his voice faintly trembles with emotion, very endearing, but it's only because I intimidate him. Unless he feels something like desire but is not aware of it? With him, my hope (too binding, alas) is to play some kind of initiatory role.

Saturday 10

I wake up at half past five, thinking I've heard the phone ring (a dream, in my opinion) and am instantly plunged back into the world of passion that was mine six months ago. (So I conclude that I am not as much in that world now.) Then I have a dream in which I run with incredible lightness (very positive, therefore) down a set of stairs with wide-spaced risers that lead to a parking lot below. But then an awful dream, I'm on the train to Rouen, to Paris. It's supposed to let me off in Yvetot. Sitting in the compartment, with another woman on my left, I read *Marie Claire*. It is night. The train stops. I search in vain for the name of the station. In the train, there are groups, Club Med–style, traveling to Italy (a reference to my trip to Rome in '63?). They get off and I do too. I don't know where I am and never will find out. All I'm told is that the next train to Paris is in eight days. So I have to find another means of travel, with truckers, for example. I ask one man, who is *huge*. His head almost touches the ceiling of the station, and I am infinitely small (very, very astonishing to me). It might be possible. I wake up.

Saw Yeltsin on *Apostrophes*, with Zinoviev. Yeltsin is S, but twenty years older. Deep-set eyes, cunning and cruel. A different mouth. The same narcissism and boastfulness—the Russian character? This morning, I regret having sent S a card.

Monday 12

Dreamed again that I was in the RER. Obscure. Will I be on public transport every single night?

Tuesday 13

I get up early to do the preface on the Tour de France, and I idle about daydreaming. The old familiar trap: desire runs wild and churns out a new story (about the "charming young man," of course). I had a dream about a trip to Annecy or Moscow, a hotel, a room whose number I've forgotten—is it 1520 or 1522? It seems to be *1520*. There's a guide with me but he's not S. And this disturbing dream: a little girl in a swimsuit has disappeared (and is then found dead?). The story is reenacted with the little girl, who is *alive* and goes out for a walk. The fact that she's alive again will make it possible for us to learn what happened. But it's very difficult because *we know the outcome*. (Very true.) The dream is the perfect embodiment of the novelistic genre, of writing, that is: we know how it ends.

Thursday 15

The charming young man came over, very much in awe, and I thought he must have fantasized too, or thought that I desired him and that he was obliged to "reciprocate" (it's me who dominates here). Atmosphere very heavy and charged, then he finds the strength to speak and it dissipates. Basically, I no longer found him desirable, he's too nosy, too much of a kid, and I've got work to do before *Apostrophes*. He stayed for over three hours. When he leaves, he tells me that his girlfriend is off skiing. Too late. I drive him to the station, and when we say goodbye, I give him the hint of a caress on his arm, but not really. It's better than nothing, enough to feed his infatuation. Slightly perverse of me. I'm sure he is very bad in bed.

At one point, he gets up from his chair. "Excuse me, I'm feeling a little stiff." I want to laugh—stiff, are you? What a difference from the absolute desire I felt for S in Leningrad.

Monday 19

I am rereading *The Mandarins*. I am so much like Anne with Lewis (that is, with S), it makes me cry. S de Beauvoir writes "No one will say 'Anne' with that accent anymore." I wrote those words too. And they came true. The days that have passed since my return from Abu Dhabi have taken me a long way from the first excruciating grief. But I just have to read passages from last year, or a few months ago, to break down in tears. And I see such a resemblance with S de B in the way I react, including my bluntness: "What a lot of trouble just to not get laid!" That's something I might have written. The last closing words, "Who knows? Maybe I'll be happy again one day." I repeat them to myself, while accepting that the happiness won't be with S. To reread *The Mandarins* made me really want to write about this passion, without cheating.

Thursday 22

Tomorrow, *Apostrophes*, which really feels to me like the exam for my Bachelor's degree or the *agrég*: there's the same feeling of "ready or not"—of getting it over with, whatever happens. Furious with myself at having only asked for 3,000 francs from Messidor, who is no doubt willing to part with more. Messidor and the PCF are closing in more and more and I find it oppressive.

Saturday 24

It's over. Why do always I have this feeling of defilement when I go on TV—being seen, and not saying everything I had to say about Beauvoir? Extreme dissatisfaction.

The truth of what I said to a woman in Bezons: my mother had to die and I to write about her, to finally "be" her.

The Salon du livre. What if S were there, with the Russian writers? *And what if he didn't want to see me* or had another woman in Paris? I'm back in last year's hell and I'm not sure I want it anymore.

Sunday 25

Extreme fatigue. Had a dream whose meaning is quite clear, about the cellar in Yvetot, and a cigarette for which I'm stubbornly searching, in spite of the risk (is it the war? or a film about the war in which I'm acting?), the name of Stalin repeated over and over. It's the cellar of 1952, my father wanting to kill my mother, the crack in my world. And Stalin is the PC (I had a friendly discussion with the Communists in Bezons yesterday). My father is class-consciousness, the impossibility of denying one's origins. The knowledge that this act I couldn't understand at twelve (but that's not so, I knew it could be explained) had its foundations: my mother's aggressiveness, her desire to rise in the world, the absolute dominion she wished to have over everyone.

Monday 26

Now I'm deprived even of my pain. Everything is gray. S will not learn that I appeared on *Apostrophes*—for him, of course. I've stopped learning Russian, and everything connected to the story of last year has lost all *meaning*: All I see is passion stripped of will, but things could not have been otherwise. And that is what is awful. *Real* life is in passion, with the desire for death. And that life is not creative. Nothing, when I think of it, could have been more sobering than the weeks spent rereading Beauvoir and Sartre. As usual I put my whole life, all my sensitivity into my comments on Beauvoir. The way in which they were reduced to anecdote by the men on the show was very upsetting.

Tuesday 27

At ten to eight this evening, the telephone rings. I answer—no one on the line. There were no more calls. A night of yearning for the "charming young man," who at the moment is the only prospect of fulfillment for my desire for love and forgetting. I also saw, in a raw and clear-cut manner, our way of making love, that of S and me. It caused me no suffering, was very close to how it was in reality. The erotic power of our connection appeared to me, its only truth, perhaps. I have been feeling bad since Saturday. First came the irrepressible urge to sleep (in the past two days) and since yesterday, a total absence of desire and of projects.

Afternoon. For the first time, I dare to do Tarot on the Minitel. I asked "Will S, my last lover, contact me soon?" The reply that arrives, half an hour later (along with the bill!): "S is certainly much younger than yourself. He'll probably get in touch, but don't expect too much from the relationship." The "psychic" was aware of my age, but still it's disturbing. No . . . to be rational (aside from the fact that she "saw" the age of S), she probably takes me for a girl who's been sleeping around and consequently (from the point of view of standard morality) won't be able to meet a "good" dependable guy.

Thursday 29

The pain of last November was revealing. It foretold everything that followed: not only a life reduced to the mere passage of time, but one in which S, the time of S, would seem almost shameful, a waste of energy. The words I said to him seem strange, now: "Anywhere, any time, ask me anything, and I'll do it for you." I'm no longer sure it's true. And yet he may still believe it.

It's the first time in my life that I've seen the trees bloom in March (they've been this way for over a week), even the lilac. No word from little B, who by now must have received my letter, which called for a reply. Anyway, I think he's so tormented and intellectual that sex with him can't be the kind of celebration I like it to be.

As expected, Abu Dhabi, *Apostrophes*, the preface for Messidor, in other words, everything with a close or distant tie with S, has propelled me away from him, from his memory. Little B is within the realm of possibility, still.

I'm no longer sure that freedom exists in writing. I even wonder if writing isn't the domain of greatest alienation, in which the past and the horror of lived experience return. But on the other hand, the result, a book, can function as a means of freedom for others.

Evening. The terrible thing is that in the past I looked for a man to "stabilize me," to have a kind of brotherly love. Now all I want from a man is love, that is, the thing which most resembles writing—the loss of self, the experience of emptiness being filled.

Friday 30

Dreamed that I had to go to Madrid (?). Tried in vain to remember the name of that model teacher I had in '59 at the École Marie-Houdemard. There was a time (when did it end?) when I probably could have produced this name at will. That time is gone.

Saturday 31

I won't be going to Madrid but to Cincinnati, and maybe New York and Chicago, in May. I was nodding off over some green beans I was picking through when they called. Jubilation, which subsides, but one of the few things that can still *grab* me is knowledge of the world. It shall be said that the place I would have been happiest to go, the USSR, is denied me. But I'm no longer sure it would make me as happy as all that. With great sadness I see the image of S turn in upon itself and revert to that of the flashy young Soviet whom I first saw at Irène's.

Think back to Spinoza: desire eternally flees toward objects, has no clear form. A work makes things *fixed*. I'm still stuck on the desire to write a historical book, but wouldn't I do better to squarely face this problem of writing and my love affair with S?

April
Sunday 1st

Dreamt that little B called me, infinitely trembling like the last time I saw him. But he violently reproaches me for my gesture of the other day. And indeed, I don't think he feels any desire for me, my last letter to him having gone unanswered. (Writing this, I hope things are otherwise, and that too is possible; maybe, for instance, he doesn't know how to go about things, "make his move.")

Am repelled by this piece I have to write for *Les cahiers pédagogiques*.* Ruined time, a waste of writing time—nothing about it leads to new knowledge.

Monday 2

Dreamt that S wrote to me in French. It wasn't easy to decode. He thanked me for my card from Abu Dhabi, men-

---

* *Les cahiers pédagogiques*, a teaching and educational sciences journal founded in 1945, published eight times a year by the Cercle de recherche et d'action pédagogiques.

tioned the difficulties he's had since his return to the USSR. In this dream I said to myself: "Look at me, imagining that I'm dreaming when I'm actually awake!"

Today I'll pick up where I left off working on my book, hoping after more than a month away to realistically assess the possibility of continuing.

Tuesday 3

I dream that my ex-husband is in my study and says, "You leave your papers out for all the world to see, you no longer put any of it away, these things that are so—" (what word does he use? "terrible"? "traumatic"?). The paper in question is my account of June '52, which I wrote down yesterday for the first time ever. "My father tried to kill my mother." A sort of initial narrative, a prelude to all the rest. Tears rose to my eyes from '52, thirty-eight years ago, soon—and then nothing. The surprise of not remembering everything, only a few words of my mother's, "Father Lecœur is listening." My father's, addressed to me: "I didn't do anything to *you*!" My own: "You'll make me miss my exam, you'll breathe disaster on me" (a Normandy expression which means that things will never be the same again, now that we have sunken into horror).

Friday 6

Return from Haute-Savoie and Grenoble.
A neutral, emotionless view of Annecy. I see "La Roseraie"

and it seems to me that I could simply push the gate open, go up the steps, enter the glassed-in porch, that is, act and *be* as if sixteen years had not passed and the same life were carrying on as then. I walked down rue Sainte-Claire: the Vidon tripe shop, little cafés, Le Fréti, and the Crémerie Pollet are still there, but not the bar run by Arabs, nor the Alsatian charcuterie (from long ago), nor the perfume counter whose owner may have earned her living from trysts with men. Le lézard vert leather goods has disappeared, as well as the Saveco supermarket on rue Filâterie. From Aix to Grenoble, little gardens can be glimpsed behind the houses. Men in caps and blue work overalls were sunning themselves on chairs in these little gardens.

I get home shattered (by the event in Grenoble, where I played my public self, the nice lady writer explaining her books), and there is nothing and never will be anything from S in the mail, nothing from little B either, end of story.

Monday 9

For the first time since November 6 (the last time I saw S), I waken with an inexplicable feeling of happiness. However, the fact that this happiness is unfounded dampens my enthusiasm, if only a little. Still, I know I'll have to decide to write one thing and not another, to stop wavering.

There is this need I have to write something that puts me in danger, like a cellar door that opens and must be entered, come what may.